DRAGON BLOOD

LINSEY HALL

For Regena and Charles, with love.

1

E ver have one of those Friday nights that's so exciting people get jealous?

Yeah, me neither.

Occasionally, I hunted demons on Friday nights. That's not so much exciting as it is deadly. But this Friday night?

My sister and I were working late, cooking up a blood sorcery potion for our buddy Aethelred, an old seer who favored blue velour tracksuits and looked like Gandalf on his way to jazzercise. Our workshop smelled of herbs and fire, and Aethelred was camped out in a chair by the hearth. Mari and I were bustling around, collecting ingredients for the potion he'd come to buy.

"How's it going over there?" he asked, having just finished regaling us with tales of the drama that had gone down at Black Bingo yesterday.

Such an exciting Friday night.

"We're getting there," Mari said.

She was dressed in her usual plunging black dress with midnight bouffant hair and a massive sweep of black eye makeup. Her disguise made her look like Elvira, Mistress of the

Dark, and even Aethelred, one of her closest friends, had never seen her without it.

I was wearing mine too—sleek white silk, but pants instead of a dress. White was a strange choice when you worked with splashing potions half the time and killed demons the other half, but it worked for me. Also I had a spell that kept my clothes pristine, since there was no way I was going to handwash silk all the time.

"I can't believe he comes to us for this stuff," I muttered to Mari.

"What?" She gave me a mock innocent look, but was barely stifling laughter. "He trusts us!"

"Enough to make his date-night potions, apparently." I dumped a vial of Heppenworth oil into the small silver cauldron. We never said *directly* what this potion was for, but all three of us knew it was to help out Gandalf's staff.

Magic sparked in the air as the ingredients swirled together. Aethelred droned on in the background—though, to be honest, I *did* like his stories. Black Bingo could be wild sometimes. Some of the witches got *real* pissed if they thought you were cheating, then shit got real.

"Ready?" Mari hovered her hand over the cauldron.

"Yep." I placed my hand next to hers, letting the steam waft up over my palm.

In tandem, we used our sharp thumbnails to slice our fingers, each letting a droplet of blood splash into the potion. Mine was white and hers was black. Though we both had dragon blood in our veins, I honestly had no idea why our blood was different colors.

Or, not red.

Purple smoke wafted up from the cauldron, smelling of lavender and wasabi. I wrinkled my nose.

"Whew, that's weird," I murmured.

"No kidding." Mari withdrew her hand, and I followed suit.

The small wounds on our fingers would close up within seconds, which was handy considering how important our blood was to our business.

"Almost done here, pal," Mari said to Aethelred.

I grabbed an empty vial off the shelf and began to funnel the potion into the glass. I was just putting the stopper in when an alarm began to blare, loud and fierce. I jumped, nearly spilling the potion. Crimson magic sparked along the ceiling.

Shit.

Red alert.

My heart rate spiked.

"Time to go!" Mari hurried to Aethelred and pulled him out of the chair.

"What's happening, Mordaca?" he sputtered, using the name that my sister gave to the world.

I corked the bottle, miraculously managing not to spill a drop. "Nothing important." I hurried to Aethelred and shoved the vial into his hands. "You can pay us later. Bye!"

Mari grabbed his arm and rushed him toward the door, leaning close to ask him in a falsely cheery voice, "Are we on for our walk tomorrow?"

She was trying to act normal, but even Aethelred would be able to tell that her voice was a bit funny. This was the second red alert this week, and that was really freaking weird. The Council of Demon Slayers usually only called on us about once a month. It varied, since demons escaped the Dark World at random times, but twice in a week was unheard of.

I waited impatiently for her to get back, drumming my fingers on the corner of the big table that sat in the center of the room.

Ten seconds later, she raced in, eyes wild. "Try explaining that to a seer!"

"No thanks." Even Aethelred didn't know we were demon slayers or Dragon Bloods. We kept that part of our lives secret. The Order of the Magica had once captured us and tried to use us for our power, and we'd never let that happen again "Now come on."

She joined me at the table, pressing her hand to one corner while I pressed mine to another. Magic ignited in the air, a pale glitter of light, and the table levitated, moving across the floor to reveal an invisible trapdoor beneath.

Silently, we walked toward the spot on the floor that was right next to the trapdoor—we had it memorized by now—and each used our sharp thumbnails to pierce our fingers again. Droplets of ebony and white blood fell to the stone ground, and magic snapped against my skin.

The floor disappeared, and Mari raced down the spiral staircase. Heart pounding, I followed close at her heels, descending into the damp earth and following the pale glow.

We reached the first platform and let the aerlig vines wrap around us as we pressed our still-bleeding fingers to one of the thick green stalks. The vines read our intentions and then let us pass.

One of them slapped me on the butt, which was all too normal.

"Watch it!" I snapped, racing down toward the Lights of Truth that sparkled on the second level.

The glittering lights brushed warmly against my skin as they spoke in my mind.

Do you mean harm?

They'd barely gotten the question out before we both said, "No."

They approved and let us pass, retracting from the space in front of us, clearing the passage. I raced after Mari, finally reaching the underground chamber that glowed with a faint blue light from the pool that glittered invitingly in the middle.

The Pool of Truth was how we maintained contact with the Council of Demon Slayers. I kicked off my shoes and gripped Mari's hand, stepping into the cold water and stopping when it lapped at my ankles.

Together, we chanted, "Here we be, let us see."

Glittering blue magic swirled in the air, moving faster and faster, a sparkling tornado that nearly blinded me. The air popped, and the magic disappeared.

An ephemeral figure rose from the middle of the pool.

I looked anxiously at her. "Hello, Agatha."

Agatha was our contact with the Council of Demon Slayers, and she looked like a cross between a ghost and a person.

"Aerdeca. Mordaca." She nodded at us. "I'm glad to see that you actually wore clothing this time."

Last time, she'd caught me while sleeping and I'd raced down here in my panties.

"I'd have come in my underwear if I'd known you'd be so disappointed." I grinned, knowing I shouldn't bait Agatha but unable to help myself. Stress made me crack bad jokes.

She shot me a pissed-off look, irritation vibrating from her. "There's a problem in Magic's Bend."

That sobered me right up. "What kind of problem?"

"Dark magic on Factory Row. A lot of it."

Shit. Our friends lived in the cool, renovated part of town full of old factories that housed apartments, antique stores, and coffee shops.

"Where did it come from?" Mari asked.

"It's a demonic signature, but we don't know where from exactly," Agatha said. "From the strength of it, we assume that whoever is responsible is from the Dark World."

Not good. There were many parts of the underworld—most

of which were associated with earthly religions—but one of the worst was the Dark World. It was a place made of pure evil. Because demons could be hired as mercenaries, the person who had orchestrated the attack could be from anywhere.

"Is there anything else you can tell us?" I asked.

Her expression turned stark. "No. Which is why this is so bad. We have no idea what's going on."

The obvious worry on her face sent a chill down my spine. "We're on it."

"We'll report back soon," Mari said.

"Godspeed." Agatha disappeared, her shimmery form sinking down into the pool.

I shared one brief look with Mari, then we sprinted out of the pool and grabbed our shoes. I beat her to the stairs, racing up them two at a time. I moved so fast that the handsy aerlig vine didn't even manage an ass-slap.

When we reached the workshop, we quickly pressed our fingertips to the corners of the wooden table. It shifted into place over the invisible trapdoor.

I met her gaze. "Meet you in the foyer in two?"

She nodded and raced off to her apartment. I sprinted toward mine. We lived in a series of three townhouses right next to each other and all connected through the inside. Our main workspace and public function area was the center one. That's where we did our blood sorcery, the business that made most of our money. Our personal houses were accessible on either side. Almost no one realized that we didn't live in the main house, and we liked it that way.

I slammed into my apartment. The all-white space was normally soothing. But not now. Nothing would be soothing until I got to Factory Row and figured out what the hell was going wrong—and if my friends were okay.

I sprinted into my bedroom, spotting the black lump of hellcat curled up in the tiny bathroom sink.

"Wally, I'm going out." I stripped out of my nice clothes and put on my fight wear—sturdy pants and a top, along with a leather jacket. All were white, my signature color, and would help me turn invisible at the blink of an eye. I called it my ghost suit. "There's a problem on Factory Row."

The black cat raised its head, smoke wafting around its form. He blinked red eyes that flickered with flame. A second later, he went back to sleep.

My new familiar had moved in a couple days ago and hadn't actually left the sink since then, except for the occasional trip out to find some dinner. He refused all tuna and cat food in favor of souls, though I hadn't seen him actually eat one.

Frankly, I'd really rather not.

Properly dressed and ready to kick ass, I ran from the room and out into the main foyer of the central townhouse. Mari sprinted in at the exact same moment, wearing an outfit identical to mine, except black.

She held out her hand for me. I gripped it tightly, ready to transport to our friends' neighborhood.

Normally, we'd drive to Factory Row. But at that moment, speed was important. It was worth Mari using her transportation magic, even though it was a finite resource. All magic was, and if we used up our stash, we'd have to rest to recoup.

A second later, the ether sucked me in, spinning me through space in a wild ride that made my stomach turn and my head pound. A second later, the ether spat us out in front of Ancient Magic, the shop run by the FireSouls. Cass, Nix, and Del were some of my very few friends.

It was dead quiet, with the exception of the crowd at the far end of the street. About a hundred and fifty yards away, there were police barricades across the road, and people were pressed up against them, rubbernecking at the entrance to Factory Row.

But we were alone on the street.

"The cops aren't in here," Mari said.

"Or the Order of the Magica." I frowned, searching the street and spotting a new statue in the park on the other side of the road. It was a stone sculpture of a jogger. Weird. That hadn't been here yesterday when we'd visited Connor and Claire at Potions & Pastilles, the coffee shop/bar that they ran down the street.

"Cowards," Mari muttered.

I couldn't help but agree. The local and national magical governments were much more red-tape oriented than we were. If something iffy was going down, they'd make sure it was good and safe for their investigators before they came in.

Which was why the Council of Demon Slayers had come to us. We made it our mission to jump into dangerous shit without looking. Not the safest, but ninety-nine percent effective.

I turned toward Ancient Magic and peered through the window. The space was cluttered with shelves and objects, magic seeping out through the glass, but I could make out no movement. There were three big statues in there as well. Weird. The FireSouls usually dealt in smaller objects, finding and selling the magic from ancient artifacts from all over the world.

Cass, Nix, and Del used their dragon-given gift to find artifacts that contained valuable magic. There was a twist, though. They only took the artifacts with the oldest magic—the ones that were about to decay entirely. Once the magic decayed, it exploded, wreaking havoc that could destroy entire archaeological sites or towns.

They brought the artifact back to their shop where the conjurer, Nix, created an exact replica. She transferred the dangerous magic into the replica, which they sold. I was a frequent customer, actually. The original artifact was put back at the archaeological site. They even had government permits.

"Let's check it out." Mari pushed open the door to the shop.

I stepped in, immediately hit by a variety of magical signatures that lit up all of my senses. There were hundreds, each replica possessing its own unique magic that gave off a distinct signature.

My gaze went immediately to the statues, which were way out of place.

Oh, shit.

"Those look familiar." Horror echoed in Mari's voice.

My limbs chilled as I approached.

"Oh no." Tears pricked my eyes as I looked at the faces of my three friends, frozen in stone.

They didn't look scared or shocked or anything. It just looked like they were having a conversation.

"What the hell happened?" Mari asked.

"I have no idea." I reached out with my magic, trying to figure out if there was any weird dark magic in the air. It was nearly impossible, though, with the signatures of the enchanted replicas filling up the space.

"There's more." Mari's voice cut through the fog in my head, and I turned to look in the direction she pointed. Three men sat on chairs in the corner. Scratch that. Three statues. They'd clearly been mid-conversation as well. Immediately, I recognized Aidan, Roarke, and Ares, the significant others of the FireSouls.

My stomach turned. All six of them.

I drew in a deep breath, trying to settle my stomach. "Let's go check Potions & Pastilles."

I gave my friends one last look, dread filling me, then turned and left, hurrying down the street toward the coffee shop. The statue in the park caught my eye again, and I realized that it wasn't a new piece of artwork.

It was a person.

My chest felt like it was full of lead as I turned toward P & P. The interior glowed with warm light as usual, but I spotted the statue behind the counter before I could even open the door.

"Shit." I pushed open the door, my skin iced with fear.

Connor stood behind the counter, his hands raised to the espresso machine. There were three patrons, all of whom sat frozen in their chairs, their bodies turned to stone. Two of them had coffee cups raised to their lips, and the other was reading the paper.

I met Mari's stark gaze. All of the color had washed out of her face.

"What's happening?" she whispered.

"I have no idea." But I could feel the dark magic more strongly here. "It's got to be a curse of some kind."

I approached Connor, my gaze pinned to his stone form. "It happened suddenly—none of them look like they expected something bad to happen. They're in the middle of doing normal things."

"So it was one quick event that turned them to stone."

"Yep." Good news, too, because I didn't want to slowly turn to stone by being here. Whatever had gone wrong, it had already happened. "But where is Claire?"

"I'll check the back." Mari hurried behind the counter and through the door that led to the little kitchen. I touched Connor's stone shoulder—probably the first time I'd ever touched him, actually—and turned to look at the coffee shop patrons.

My gaze snagged on a note pinned to a little corkboard near the door.

Emergency, headed to San Fran. 10 p.m.

--Claire

I pulled it off the wall and followed Mari to the back.

"She's not here," Mari said. "Maybe her apartment above the shop."

I held up the note. "She left last night. This wasn't here when we came for a drink."

"You noticed?"

I nodded.

Mari dug her tiny phone out of a secret pocket and dialed. She stared at the phone, her brow creased. It went to voice mail. "She's not picking up."

"Damn." Four out of five friends, frozen solid. Along with at least four other people. I had a feeling that if I checked all the shops and apartments in the vicinity, people would be frozen there as well.

Mari's nose wrinkled, and she started sniffing like a bloodhound on the scent. She turned to face the back door. "You smell that?"

I sniffed. Rotten eggs and sour milk.

Connor and Claire would never have those in their kitchen.

"Dark magic." I followed the scent, headed to the door.

It led out to an alley, and I followed it to the right, winding through the narrow space and into a larger courtyard between two of the factory buildings.

"I didn't even realize this was here," Mari said.

There was a scattering of trees, dumpsters, and a single bench, along with a glowing crystal thing that sat right in the middle. The stench of dark magic emanated from it—rotten eggs and sour milk.

I pointed at the crystal. "That can't be normal."

"Ah, no." Mari frowned and approached it. "What the hell is it?"

I followed her to the crystal, raising my shirt up over my mouth and nose. It didn't help much.

We stopped a few feet in front of it, squinting into the glowing red depths. It was about the size of a soccer ball, waist high and sitting on top of a post that plunged deep into the ground.

A stick lay nearby, fallen off one of the trees. I picked it up and moved it toward the glowing orb.

"Are you sure you want to do that?" Mari asked.

"Not really, no."

She chuckled.

I sucked in a deep breath and poked the orb with the stick. A shock traveled up the wood, into my arm. Pain flared, and I dropped the stick, jumping back.

"You okay?" Mari frowned at me.

I shook my hand. "Fine. But that thing is stuck on there, solid."

"It has to be the cause of the problems here." Mari crouched down, inspecting it closer. "But *how*?"

"I don't know. I don't think we should destroy it, though."

"No, agreed. What if it makes the stone spell permanent?"

"My fear exactly."

The sound of voices filtered toward us from a nearby alley. It was probably the police or the Order of the Magica coming to check it out, and they'd boot us as soon as they saw us. Or decide that we were responsible and take us into custody.

I looked at Mari. "We need more time to investigate."

"Use your ghost suit to turn invisible and look around. I'll try to hold them off."

"How?"

She shrugged. "I'll figure it out."

She didn't have the power of invisibility like I did. This suit had cost me a hell of a lot of money and magic. But she was resourceful.

"Safe hunting," I said.

She squeezed my shoulder quickly. "Safe hunting."

I drew my hood up, letting the invisibility overtake me, then began to scour the courtyard. I needed something—anything—that would tell me where the damned orb had come from. What it could do. Who had put it here.

For the most part, the entire place was empty. Just rocks and twigs, shadows and nothing. The voices stopped, though. Somehow, Mari had stalled them.

I'd finished scouring the square with no luck when a figure entered from the same alley we had.

Declan.

The tall, broad-shouldered fallen angel looked as good as ever. His dark hair was disheveled, in the way of a perfectly done-up clothing model. Except I knew he didn't waste time on his hair. Or on his face, with his full lips, dark eyes, and once-broken nose. All of his good looks were natural, damn him.

I'd last seen Declan a few days ago after our kiss. And after I'd tried to enchant him to forget I existed.

It hadn't worked.

And he'd realized what I was up to.

He had *not* been pleased.

We'd parted ways, and I hadn't expected to see him again. It was disappointing, actually, even though I'd been the one to screw things up. But I hadn't wanted to get close to anyone—not if it meant they could find out what I really was.

He'd said it was foolish to hang around a woman who would try to remove herself from his memory anyway. He had a point.

But what the hell was the bounty hunter doing here?

Was he after me?

2

Q uickly, Declan swept his gaze over the square, missing me entirely. I stood stock-still in the shadows, my invisibility suit helping me avoid detection.

He frowned when he spotted the orb. Unlike Mari and me, he didn't approach immediately. Instead, he circled the square, looking for clues or dangers.

He didn't find anything, though he nearly ran into me. I moved back silently, heart pounding.

Should I reveal myself?

No.

One, I was too curious to see what he would do.

Two, he was probably still pissed at me.

He approached the sphere, curiosity and worry gleaming in his dark eyes. He looked at the stick that I'd tossed on the ground.

Would he pick it up?

He ignored it.

Points for the clever angel.

He knelt next to the orb, digging into his pocket. After a moment, he withdrew a tiny silver pebble, then held it up to the orb. He was careful not to touch the gleaming surface, but he held it quite close.

I crept nearer, wanting to get a good view.

The orb pulsed and glowed, the red magic growing active. Excited. Tiny crimson sparkles drifted toward the silver pebble that Declan held. Slowly, it turned red as well, a tiny bit of the magic of the orb transferring to the pebble.

Nice.

The pebble was a magic collector. They were rare and expensive. I'd only ever made one a couple of times. He wouldn't be able to suck all the magic out of the orb—not even close— but he could get a sample of it.

I was nearly to him when I stopped dead in my tracks. I'd been so absorbed by his actions that I hadn't realized how close I was getting. I held my breath.

"Something to go on, at least," he muttered.

He was going to track the magic in the sphere, and right now, it was the only clue he had. The only clue *I* had. I doubted I'd find anything else in the square if I checked again.

Declan reached into his pocket, and my heart thundered. When I spotted the gray stone, I grinned.

A transport charm.

I was only about six feet from him. That would give me enough time.

Declan hurled the stone to the ground, and a burst of gray glittery dust rose high in the air. He stepped into it, and I followed, sprinting for the temporary portal.

As the one who had thrown the transport charm, he'd be able to choose where it went. I'd just hitch a ride and follow along.

I made it to the glittery cloud before it dissipated, and the ether sucked me in, twisting me through space as it sent me toward...somewhere. I had no idea.

When it spat me out on a cobblestone street, I stumbled, trying to keep my footsteps silent, and inspected my new surroundings.

Declan was already walking down a narrow, winding street ahead of me. He turned back to look at me, his brow furrowed.

I froze, breath held.

His gaze met mine—almost. He couldn't see me, but I felt the connection. A tingle down my spine. Did he feel it, too?

He shook his head and turned back, striding off down the street. I hurried to keep up, years of practice keeping my footsteps silent. The air was cold and dark here, with fog lying heavy on the ground. It was an old city—some of the buildings on this narrow street looked to be medieval.

English, probably. The air was moist enough, and some of the construction looked Tudor, with the signature dark wood and white plaster. Old iron lamps rose tall along the street, casting a yellow glow upon the fog. The shops were full of normal things—clothes, shoes, stationery, books. No potions or weapons or shrunken heads.

So we were probably in a human town. Maybe a mixed human and supernatural town.

Declan knew where he was going, though. He moved quickly down the street, his long strides eating up the ground. I pressed my fingertips to the comms charm around my neck, muting it in case Mari decided to call me while I was on the hunt.

A couple hundred yards later, we passed onto another street —this one was a bit wider, with a massive sandstone cliff on one side. I couldn't see it, but I'd bet a hundred bags of Cheetos that there was a castle on that cliff. I did spot a smallish stone tower perched there, which only confirmed my theory.

Magic sparkled in the air, and I caught sight of a shop

window that featured broomsticks and cauldrons, along with spell books.

Supernatural part of town.

A sign above the shop read, *Nottingham's Niceties and Notteties.*

So we were in Nottingham. Wasn't that somewhere outside of London? Or kind of close? At least by American distance standards.

Declan beelined for a pub that appeared to be built into the side of the cliff. Parts of the building protruded from the rock walls—a couple of walls and a half roof—but most of the pub was set deep into the earth. Light glittered through the mullioned glass windows, revealing patrons of all species—fae, shifter, Magica, even a goblin.

I followed Declan toward the pub, which was called Ye Olde Trip to Brigadoon.

What a mouthful.

Thankfully, the door was propped open to let in some fresh air, and I was able to slip in behind him.

It was late at night here, but the whole place was packed, with supernaturals standing shoulder to shoulder. It was a maze of tiny rooms, and the ceiling above was rough golden stone. A small bar was built near the door, and Declan leaned against it.

The bartender was a pretty woman with a truly magnificent chest. She knew it, too, and wore a low-cut tank top that made her breasts look like a work of art. Especially when she crossed her arms and leaned over, batting her eyes at Declan.

I looked down at my little boobs and mouthed, "Don't worry, guys. You're fab, too."

A fairy next to me frowned and tilted her head, purple eyes confused. No doubt she'd heard the barest hint of my whisper, but I'd been so quiet she couldn't have heard much more. She shook her head, purple wings on her back quivering just slightly from the movement of her shoulders.

I looked toward Declan, perking my ears to hear what he had to say.

"Hello, Lira." His voice was low and smooth, sending a shiver over my spine.

I kind of wanted to *be* Lira right now.

No, moron. You had your chance.

"Declan," she purred. "Long time, no see."

"A total tragedy, it is."

"We could go, ah, see more of each other in the back." She pointed toward an alcove at the rear of the bar.

Wow, she wasted no time.

"As much as I'd love to, I'm on a job."

I scowled, then mentally kicked myself.

"You're here to see Aurelia the All Knowing?" She raised a brow.

"Indeed I am. Is she open to visitors?"

"To you, she is."

Jeez, what was with this guy? Panties seemed to be flung into the air wherever he walked. Mine included, which was embarrassing.

"You're a gem. Thanks, Lira."

She smiled. "You know where to find me."

"You know where to find me," I muttered under my breath. Yeah, I was childish. It wasn't my finest moment.

Declan turned and walked through the crowd. A normal person would have to do some pushing and squishing, the way mortals got through a packed place. Not the fallen angel, though. People parted like the freaking Red Sea for him.

I hurried after him, taking advantage of the temporary spaces within the crowd. At the back of the bar, Declan found a staircase leading up. A burly man guarded it, his arms crossed over his chest and his brow set in a scowl. The faint blue tinge to his skin was weird—I'd never seen a supernatural like that.

Without a word, he stepped aside for Declan, who took the stairs two at a time. I raced forward, hoping to beat the man, but he was back at his post as soon as Declan passed.

There was no way I could sneak by.

Damn.

I melted back against the wall, finding a tiny nook to squeeze into. The whole place was a crazy maze of rooms and cubbies, carved out of the rock hundreds of years ago. I could feel the history in the air.

Quickly, I pressed my fingertip to my comms charm and whispered, "Mari?"

"Where the hell have you been?" she hissed back. "I've been trying to call you."

"I know, I know. I silenced my charm because I'm stalking Declan."

"Oh, you're stalking—" There was a brief pause as she processed. "You're what?!"

"He found a clue and I didn't, so I'm trying to figure out what he does."

"Fine, that's not a bad plan."

"I only have a sec. What are you doing?"

"The voices that we heard while we were in Factory Row belonged to Order Investigators. They don't know what the orb is, but they know it's dangerous."

"Duh."

"Preach. Anyway, they've determined that it's too dangerous to approach, so they are bringing in a specialist team from Europe to do an assessment."

"That'll take *forever*." The Order was famous for the slowness of their operations. They were nearly crippled under bureaucracy and were notoriously corrupt. We didn't trust them as far as we could throw them, and we had very good reason. "That leaves this up to us."

"Sure does. By the time they get their shit together, we'll have solved it or we'll *all* be dead."

"Fine, then I've got to go follow Declan."

"I'm off to San Francisco. If I can get closer to Claire, my Seeker sense might kick in and I can find her."

"Good." Maybe she'd have a clue. And since she was pretty much our only friend who hadn't turned into a rock—besides Aethelred, the old seer—I wanted to know she was okay. "Safe hunting."

"Safe hunting."

I cut the connection on the comms charm and stepped forward. I wouldn't need to become visible for this. In fact, it would help if I weren't. Quickly, I slipped through the crowd, avoiding the people who filled the bar.

The guard at the stairs hadn't moved an inch. I sliced my finger with my sharp thumbnail. Blood welled, and I swiped the white liquid over his forehead and yanked my hand away. He flinched, slapping a hand to his face.

"Move to the side for three seconds," I whispered, imbuing the magic with the power of suggestion. I definitely preferred using this magic while I was invisible and no one could see me.

He frowned, then stepped aside briefly, pressing his shoulder against the wall. I slipped past him and up the stairs, hurrying on silent feet. The hallway at the top was narrow and dark. Though there were several doors, only one glowed with light.

I made my way to it, perking my ears for any noise.

"I was hoping you could tell me what kind of spell it is." Declan's deep voice filtered down the hall. He sounded...different.

A bit the way he did when he'd flirted with me.

"Anything for you, sugar," a woman's voice purred down the hall.

Were they *flirting?*

He'd just been flirting with me, two days ago!

What a man-whore.

I scowled—I shouldn't even be *thinking* about that—and stopped in the doorway, peeking through.

A beautiful dark-skinned woman leaned over a desk, staring down at the tiny crimson orb that glowed with dark magic. Her breasts spilled out of the pink shirt she wore, giving the bartender downstairs a run for her money in the cleavage department. What was with this place? Hot-woman head-quarters?

She tapped one long fingernail on the desk as she thought.

"Let's see what we've got here." Her voice made me think of whiskey and honey.

Hell, even I wanted to flirt with her now.

She peered hard at the orb. Then slowly, she shook her head. Any flirtation or lightness on her face had disappeared. "Some dark magic in there."

"You're not afraid of a little dark magic," Declan said.

"No, honey, I'm not." The woman looked up. "But I *am* smart, and I don't want to get mixed up in any of this."

"There's no *this*." Declan raised his hands, an innocent expression on his face. He pulled it off pretty well. Probably the angel blood in him.

"Cut the crap, sugar." Her expression flattened out.

"Never could pull a fast one on you." Declan grinned. "I'll pay, of course."

Her brows rose, an interested expression on her face. "Oh?"

"With money, Nara."

"Fine." She sounded disappointed.

What else would she want him to pay with?

From the way she looked at him, I had a feeling I knew.

She nodded, lips pursed. "You'd better. Ten thousand. Cash."

I winced, but Declan nodded as if he'd expected it. "Obviously I don't have it on me."

No, he'd almost need a briefcase for that kind of dough. And damn, this guy shelled out the big bucks when he was on his bounty-hunting gigs. Did he even take home any money?

Holy fates, was he doing this out of the goodness of his *heart*?

I felt a horrified expression twist the corners of my mouth. Mari and I *never* worked like that. We always expected to be paid, and paid well.

Except for that one time. And that other time.

And right now.

Because even if Agatha hadn't told me to get to it on this job, I'd have done it because my friends were in danger.

Shit.

I leaned against the doorjamb, surprise coursing through me. I wasn't quite the person I thought I was.

I was being *nice.*

I shook my head. Screw it. Why I was doing it didn't matter, as long as I succeeded.

Despite my recent existential crisis, the scene in front of me continued to play out. My breath caught in my lungs as I watched the woman debate. Apparently she needed a little while longer to decide, or she liked keeping Declan hanging on the line.

Finally, she sighed. "All right. I'll expect the money by morning."

"Not a problem." He smiled. "Thank you, Nara."

She waved a hand. "Whatever, just pay me, pretty boy."

"Happy to."

Nara picked up the glowing orb with two fingers, a look of distaste on her face as she walked to the fireplace. I shifted my spot in the room, moving on silent feet so I could have a good view of her as she worked.

Only then did I notice that the room was an ornately decorated masterpiece. It looked like it was straight out of the Gilded Age—all fancy furniture, golden accents, and navy walls draped in silk. I was almost as interested in history as I was in marine biology. Though I mostly just read about the subjects, I still had a pretty good background. And this place screamed old money.

And it was built right into a cave, I remembered.

Wild.

Unceremoniously, Nara tossed the rock into the fire.

I reached out, a shout almost escaping my lips. I bit it back.

Declan didn't seem too concerned. Vibrating with tension, I watched Nara reach for a small jar on the marble and wood mantel. There were over a dozen, and she chose a blue one. Carefully, she sprinkled powder over the flames, turning them blue.

She returned the jar to the mantel and grabbed a red one. Her hands moved fast as she sprinkled powders of various colors on the flames, all different quantities of the sparkling stuff. The fire changed color and even smell as she worked, and her face glowed in the light of the flame.

Finally, she quit with the powders and crouched down. An image began to shimmer in the flames.

Ah, so that's what she was up to. Nara was a rare type of PyroSeer, one who was able to see images in fire.

I squinted into the flames, making out the shape of a skinny man with no hair. His eyebrows were wild, so bushy and long that they swept back almost to his ears. He muttered under his breath as his eyes blazed with an internal light. His hands, which he held up near his chest, glowed with blue light. Slowly, an orb began to form in front of him, crimson and bright.

Shit. The guy who'd made the orb that had enchanted my friends.

"Well?" Declan asked.

"Shh." Nara hissed, then squinted into the fire.

Declan shut his mouth, but I didn't blame him for asking. I was dying to know who the guy was, too. What kind of magic was he making?

Finally, Nara sat back. The image had stopped changing. "That's all I'm getting."

"Who is it?" Declan asked.

"Mauritius the Dark, a dark mage who only works for a hefty price. He was once the Arch Magus, though he was replaced by someone far more powerful."

Lachlan Munroe. I actually knew the current Arch Magus—the most powerful mage in the world—though not well. He was a decent guy. Not like this Mauritius, who made magic that turned people to stone.

"Can you tell what type of magic he's put into the sphere?"

I leaned forward, keen to hear the answer. Declan's gaze shot in my direction, and I stiffened.

Had he seen me?

No way.

But heat suffused me.

His gaze only lingered for a moment, then he looked back at Nara.

She shook her head. "Not a clue. But you can find him in Toronto."

Jackpot. I'd been right to follow Declan.

But, Toronto? That was almost an entirely human city. Very few supernaturals at all. A dark mage wouldn't normally hang out there. But then, Mauritius didn't look normal. He looked like an evil bastard who probably had a lot of supernatural enemies.

Better for him if he spent his time away from everyone else.

"Thank you, Nara." Declan moved toward the door, turning back briefly. "I'll have the money to you by tomorrow."

"See that you do." She smiled, and it was warm this time.

Declan slipped out the door, and I turned to follow.

"Wait a moment." Nara's voice was low and clear, quiet enough for only me to hear.

I stiffened, glancing back.

There was no way she could see me.

Oddly, Nara was bending toward the fireplace. She reached into the flame and grabbed a handful of fire, then hurled it at me.

It all happened so quickly I couldn't even blink. One second, she was doing something crazy like sticking her hand into a roaring fire, and the next, the ball of flame was flying toward me. I was so close that it took less than a split second to reach me, slamming into my chest.

Heat enveloped me, immobilizing me. My heartbeat thundered wildly in my head, nearly deafening.

Oh hell, I was in trouble.

3

O range fire flicked all around me. Panic flared, until I realized that it really wasn't that hot. Just really warm. I was frozen solid, bound within its grip.

Nara strolled over, interest on her face. She stopped in front of me, reaching up to flick the hood off my face.

She pursed her lips and nodded, her gaze on mine. "You're the one he likes."

"Ah, what?"

"The flame reveals all."

"About me?" What the hell was going on?

"Some about you, some about me. Some about Declan." Her gaze flicked to the door. "Who is gone, by the way. So no help is coming."

I hadn't even thought of calling out for help—it just wasn't my usual instinct—and that flame had come at me so fast that instinct was the only thing that would have helped.

Though my heart was thundering and my skin was chilled, I didn't sense a lot of danger coming off of Nara. She was a bitch, but I liked bitches. Bitches got stuff done.

I raised a brow. "Do I need help?"

"Maybe." Nara shrugged. "Why are you following Declan?"

I considered bluffing, but apparently she could see stuff in the flames. Such as the fact that he liked me, whatever the hell that meant. "That magic has turned my friends to stone. I want to turn them back. Declan has the only clue, so I'm following him."

And he was getting away. I struggled against the flames that bound me, but they held tight.

"You're connected to him somehow." She gestured to the flames that flicked around my body. "The flames never lie."

"Why the hell do you care?"

"I was curious."

"So you went straight to *fire prison*?"

"You snuck into my place of business. You're lucky I didn't hit you with some real flame."

"Thanks for that." I actually didn't want to become a barbecue special.

"I just wanted to get a look at you. See what the flames were talking about."

"They were talking about me and Declan? What were they saying?"

"That you would be together. But then torn apart."

Oh shit. That was a loaded concept. "What the hell does that mean? I hardly know him."

"I'm not sure. But it's interesting, isn't it?"

Interesting was a word for it, but mostly it just confirmed my desire to stay away from him. I couldn't trust him, and what was the point anyway, if we'd be torn apart?

Nara waved her hand. "You're free to go. And you'd better hurry, if you want to catch Declan."

The flames that bound me snapped, and suddenly, I could move. I gave Nara one last look. She stood silhouetted by the flames, a seer surrounded by the mystery of her art.

I turned and hightailed it out of there, flipping my hood up as I ran.

Declan had a lead, and I needed to catch him.

I hurried out onto the street in Nottingham, leaving the weird little cave bar behind.

Declan was gone.

And it was raining.

A cold drop of water splashed on my forehead. I darted back under an overhanging roof that had been built right into the cliff behind me.

"Shit."

Agreed. The voice sounded from below, and I looked down.

Wally looked up at me, flame red eyes burning. The smoke that formed his fur wafted in the breeze.

"You saw all that?"

He nodded. *A bit embarrassing at the end.*

"Sure was. Want to go to Toronto?"

Not really.

"No?"

It's Canada, in the winter. He sounded utterly appalled.

"Good point."

And Canadians are as nice as they seem. Most go to a nice afterlife. Not many souls hanging around for me to eat.

"Fair enough."

But if it gets exciting, I'll turn up.

"By exciting, you mean, if I almost die?"

Yep.

He was a cat of few words. "See you later, pal."

I reached into my pocket for a transport charm, and hurled it to the ground. The cloud of silver smoke burst up, and I stepped inside it, letting the ether suck me up and spin me through space. The ether spat me out on a freezing street corner in downtown Toronto.

With the time change, it was earlier in the evening here, but there still weren't many people out. Probably because it was freaking freezing. I shivered hard and tugged my jacket around me. This damned thing was better for invisibility than warmth.

All around, buildings soared high in the sky. Every single one looked super modern, all chrome and glass. Snow twinkled in the streetlights, swirling above.

Wally had been right—too cold in Toronto.

The streets themselves were wide and clean, and so empty it was almost apocalyptic. Where the hell did this Mauritius live?

I pulled my cell phone out of my pocket, grateful to see that I had a few bars left. My comms charm only worked with Mari, the person who wore its mate. Everyone else got a phone call.

I scrolled down the numbers and pulled up Ana Blackwood, my friend in Scotland and the partner of Lachlan Munroe. Maybe the current Arch Magus would know a bit about the former one.

She picked up on the fourth ring.

"Ana?" I asked.

"Do you *know* what time it is?"

"Shit o'clock?"

"Exactly." She groaned. "But it must be important. You've literally never called me."

"Can I speak to Lachlan?"

"You wake me up to speak to my boyfriend." She made a disgusted noise. "Figures."

"Thanks."

"Yeah. And good luck with whatever it is that's worth calling about. I'm there if you need me."

I smiled. She was grouchy, but she had my back. My kind of person.

"Hello?" Lachlan's voice was groggy with sleep.

"Hey, Lachlan. Got a sec?"

"I do now."

Man, these two were not cheerful risers. "Do you know where Mauritius lives in Toronto? I figured you would since you took his spot as Arch Magus."

"That weasel?"

"The very one."

"Little bastard lives in a tower downtown. Looks like a super villain's lair. Stupid, if you ask me."

Really stupid, considering that this was a mostly human city, and he'd bring the Order of the Magica down upon his head if he alerted them to the presence of magic in the world.

I looked up, scanning the horizon. More than a dozen massive buildings competed to be the tallest, but only one had a bunch of black spikes at the top. "Does his building look like it wears a big evil crown?"

"That's the one." Lachlan scoffed. "Moron. He's on the top floor, heavily guarded. Owns the whole building and sells dark magic out of it."

"Know any of his weaknesses?"

"Aye, actually. Most of his magic is stolen and stored in a vessel that he keeps near him. He uses it to do most of his work."

"Weird. What kind of vessel?"

"Don't know. Too big to carry on his person, but not enormous. Should be in his office. At least, that's the rumor. Without it, he's a normal mage with average powers. Below average, even."

"Thanks, Lachlan."

"Good luck."

I hung up and hurried across the street, hoping the run would warm up my blood. Snow pelted my face as I cut down the wide avenue toward the tower of evil. A few cars were out, but almost no people.

As I ran, I tapped my comms charm. "Mari?"

"How's it going?"

"Got a lead. You find Claire yet?"

"Still on the hunt."

"Me too."

"Safe hunting."

"Safe hunting."

As I neared the building, I slowed to a walk. They couldn't see me in my ghost suit—it was never any good for guards to spot you racing up to their boss's evil lair—but I needed to scout the lay of the land.

How would I get in? And how far ahead was Declan?

As I neared the front doors, I spotted the guards first. There were a half dozen of them, all mages. Demons, I could handle. Mages were another thing entirely. They could have any kind of magic, and six of them were risky.

Not to mention the prickly sensation that sparked along my skin.

I'd bet a vat of General Tso's chicken that the prickling feeling was a charm that would strip away my invisibility. Any evil mastermind worth their salt would have that one in their lobby.

So, the main entrance was out. I scanned the rest of the building and spotted a quieter street to the right. Away from the guards. Probably my best bet.

I sprinted over, as much to keep warm as to catch up with Declan.

A quick survey of the building revealed no doors on this side. But there was a second-floor office with a light on. The walls were made entirely of glass, and I spotted a man sitting hunched over a desk. He would do nicely.

The second part of my plan was harder. I needed something heavy that could break the window, but could also look like it'd been picked up off the street.

Except the streets were so damned clean in this city.

In the end, I had to climb a damned lamppost and pull off the heavy metal top that sat over the glass globe. In a pinch, someone might believe it had broken a window. It probably wasn't big enough or heavy enough, but I didn't need the ruse to hold for long.

I lined myself up beneath the man's window and set my chunk of metal on the ground, then called my mace from the ether. Its weight was comforting in my hand as I gripped the chain and gave the spiked ball at the end a few practice swings. Long, overhead throws like this were tricky.

Once I had it moving the way I wanted, I swung it at the second-floor glass window above. It crashed through, and I ducked as the broken glass rained down upon me.

The building alarm began to wail.

As I'd hoped, the mace had caught at the metal lip of the glass wall, providing me with a handy chain to climb up. I tossed the metal lamppost top up into the room and scrambled up the mace chain, using it as a rope.

I climbed to my feet inside the room, barely avoiding some nasty cuts from the glass. I pulled up my mace chain and stashed the weapon in the ether.

The guy at the desk stood, his messy hair askew and his eyes wide. I was invisible and so was my mace, but he'd just seen the window break and *then* the metal object had flown through a few seconds later. No wonder he was confused.

"What the hell?" He moved to the window to look out, brow creased.

I could have tried to just slip through, but this had a better chance of success. Guards could be here any minute, so I needed to work fast.

I scanned the desk behind him. It was covered in ancient

books, and his fingertips were stained with black ink. They looked like grimoires, and he was obviously working on them for Mauritius. Weird to be doing such ancient work in a modern building.

I nicked my finger with my thumbnail and let the blood rise. Quick as I could, I darted toward him and swiped my finger over his forehead. He flinched at the touch, though he couldn't see me.

I imbued my words with the power of suggestion. "A vandal threw that piece of metal through the window and ran off down the street."

Slowly, he nodded, his eyes blank.

I smiled. That would do nicely.

He sat back down at his desk to wait for the guards, and I turned to leave, making sure that my hood still covered my face, ensuring that the invisibility spell was working. I hoped that the charm that stripped invisibility was limited to the lobby. Probably was. Those things were so expensive and difficult to make that even the wealthiest didn't imbue their whole homes with them, much less a giant office building.

The halls were quiet as I left, most people having gone home for the night. I needed to get to the top floor, but where were the stairs? I'd avoid the elevator if I could help it.

I sprinted through the halls on silent feet, searching for stairs. It took me ten minutes to finally admit defeat.

"There are no freaking stairs," I muttered. What a hazard.

But it only confirmed that Mauritius was obsessive about security. If people could only use the elevator, he could monitor that. So what if there was a fire? He was a dick who didn't care if his employees burned. It wasn't like the Order of the Magica had health and safety regulations. Our magical government did a few things right, but not a lot. And I'd bet big bucks that if the human health and safety department ever made it in here—

doubtful—that he enchanted them into giving him a passing grade.

I returned to the elevator and pressed the button to go up. A red light flashed, and I noticed the card swipe.

Shit. You needed an access card to ride.

I hurried back toward the office I'd broken into. With any luck, the guards would still be there. A moment later, I rounded the hall to see them striding out of the office, annoyance on their faces.

Two mages, undetermined skill set. Both were men in their mid-twenties, looking nearly identical with buzzed blond hair and green eyes.

"Idiot kids," one muttered.

"Fucking hate vandals," said the other.

Perfect, they'd bought it.

Carefully, I made sure to get my magical signature under control, drawing it to me as I approached them. I didn't need them getting a whiff or a taste of my magic and figuring out there was someone nearby. One of them hesitated as he neared me, his gaze searching the area around my face. Then he shook his head and continued on.

I followed them to the elevator, slipping on behind them.

Come on, go tell your boss.

If they took me right to the top floor, I'd be sitting pretty.

Instead, the elevator went down.

Shit.

They got off on the bottom floor.

There was a card swipe here, too, but I pressed the button for the top floor anyway, holding my breath.

Nothing happened.

Of freaking course.

I looked up, spotting a grate in the ceiling of the elevator.

Carefully, I pushed aside the grate and climbed onto the top of the elevator. The shaft was dark and musty-smelling, rising hundreds of feet overhead.

Damn, this was going to be a long climb. I started slowly, getting the hang of it. The structural support beams for the shaft acted as handholds, and eventually I was moving a lot quicker.

Hey, this wasn't so bad.

As if fate had heard me, a rumble sounded from below. I looked down, spotting the elevator roaring up toward me.

Shit.

I pressed myself against the wall and peered back down. It was nearly to me. And there was no way that it wouldn't hit me. There was almost no space between the sides of the shaft and the elevator.

"Crap, crap, crap." Only one option.

The elevator was nearly to me when I jumped, trying to time it perfectly. I landed on the roof of the elevator with a thud, wincing.

Whoever was inside *had* to have heard that.

I lay perfectly still, not even breathing, as the grate at the top of the elevator shifted open.

Declan's head popped through. I nearly fainted from relief.

Hang on. How the hell had that bastard gotten the elevator to work?

Declan frowned, turning in a full circle. Then he shrugged and dropped back down into the compartment.

Thank fates.

I looked up, cringing when I saw how close the ceiling was. Holy fates, this elevator was unnaturally fast. We were nearly there, with no time left to crawl into the compartment.

My skin chilled as visions of being crushed like a bug flashed in my mind. Frantic, I scanned the roof of the shaft, finally spotting a small area that looked recessed. It was right overhead. I had less than a second left.

My heart thundered as I curled into a ball, as tight and small as I could go.

The elevator stopped.

I sucked in a breath. *Still alive. Not a pancake.*

But I didn't have a lot of time. The doors dinged, opening. Through the grate, I saw Declan step out. I had only seconds.

There wasn't much room, but I managed to slide the grate to the side and slip into the elevator, then out the doors just as they were closing. It was agony to keep from panting, but I held it in, slowly surveying the huge, fancy hallway.

The first thing I noticed was the prickle of a charm against my skin. I'd bet big bucks we couldn't transport directly off this floor. A common, anti-theft emergency measure.

Declan was nowhere to be seen, but there was a guard collapsed on the floor.

Damn, the fallen angel was fast.

I moved down the hall, heading toward the sound of a fight. By the time I made it to the huge office, there were four guards on the floor and a terrified little man pressed back against his office chair. He was bald, with crazy eyebrows.

Mauritius.

Declan leaned over the desk and set the tiny crimson orb on the gleaming wooden surface. "Tell me about the crimson orb in Magic's Bend. It turned people to stone, and I know you made it."

The man swallowed hard, staring up at Declan with wide eyes. "Guards are coming."

"They won't get here before I get my information."

The man cowered, and I would have felt bad for him except for the fact that his magic reeked of decay and sulfur. A supernatural's signature was an infallible clue as to the nature of his magic, and this guy was evil.

No matter how he cowered, he was still a dark magic practitioner who made dangerous spells that hurt people. Hurt my *friends.*

I crept into the room, scanning the space for the object that Lachlan had mentioned. Too big to be carried easily on his body, but probably not enormous. He'd keep it nearby.

Declan leaned farther over the desk, his voice hard. "Tell me how to stop the spell that's turned people to stone. Why did you put it there?"

"I didn't!"

I believed that, actually. Not only did he sound terrified and honest, he didn't do his own dirty work. This might not even be his plan. Lachlan had said he sold magic, and what interest would a former Arch Magus from Toronto have in Magic's Bend?

He'd sold the magic to someone, if I had to bet. And I'd get the truth as soon as I got his talisman.

I crept toward the desk. Mauritius's head snapped up and toward me, his eyes narrowing. "Who's there?"

I froze. *Shit.*

No way he could see me.

His nose twitched.

Smell?

Nah, I had my signature on lockdown.

Whatever it was, he was suspicious.

Declan turned to look, too, his brow furrowed. With his face fully turned away from Mauritius, he silently mouthed my name, "Aerdeca?"

Oh fates, the fallen angel was clever. He'd probably been suspicious for a while, and he knew about my ghost suit.

Almost immediately, he turned back to Mauritius, looming over him and raising a hand that he ignited with heavenly fire.

He was covering for me by distracting Mauritius. He had an

inkling I was here, and he was freaking *covering* so I could do my shit. I'd bet a hundred bags of Cheetos on it.

Maybe it was wishful thinking, but either way, Mauritius's eyes snapped to Declan and widened at the sight of the heavenly fire.

He was *definitely* distracted.

"The magic in the sphere," Declan said. "How does it work? How do we disable it?"

"I'm not telling." The man set his jaw.

I moved silently around the room, looking at all the knick-knacks lying on various surfaces. There were a few possibilities —a beautiful crystal on a low table in front of the window. An ancient dagger on a stand. A small book.

Maybe.

I turned toward the desk where Mauritius sat.

Declan held the flame near him. "You've endangered dozens of lives. Maybe hundreds. Don't think I won't use this to get the truth out of you."

His voice was so cold that it made even me shiver—and I was pretty much made of ice.

"You can't scare me." The man's voice wavered, but there was a thread of steel to it. "This is my business. My client paid for that magic. If I tell some damned fallen angel how to disable it, then I've betrayed my client. I'll lose them all if I do that." Mauritius's gaze dropped to a plain white coffee mug on his desk, then up to Maximus.

"Betraying just one client won't lose *all* of them," Declan said.

"You know nothing about my business." The man scowled. "These people are ruthless. There are a lot of places you can buy the magic I sell. What I *also* sell is the guarantee I won't rat them out."

"Not even to save your life?" Declan tossed the ball of flame up in the air as if it were a baseball. "Because I'd consider it a good day to get rid of scum like you."

The man's gaze dropped to the coffee mug again.

I grinned.

"Damned fallen angel." Mauritius turned pale, but crossed his arms and set his jaw.

He wasn't going to talk.

Not when his life was threatened. That wasn't valuable enough.

But his magic...

I grabbed the coffee mug off the counter, spotting the words *World's Best Boss* in block capitals. I choked on a laugh as I darted backward.

Mauritius's eyes widened as his coffee mug disappeared. Once I'd touched it, my ghost suit's magic had extended to it. Mauritius lunged upward and over the desk.

Declan grabbed him by the throat, and he choked, eyes bulging.

I flipped my hood back, appearing a few feet away from them.

Declan's gaze fell on me, and he smiled. "I thought it might be you."

4

"Thanks for covering for me while I found this." I tossed the cup into the air and caught it, watching with delight as Mauritius gulped like a fish.

Declan frowned. "What is it, exactly?"

"The source of his magic." I grinned at the former Arch Magus, making sure my voice was icy. "Isn't that right?"

"N-no idea what you're talking about," he stuttered.

"This has to be the world's stupidest mug. There's no way such a thing would mean anything to you on its own. And I have it on good authority that most of your magic is stored in a talisman."

"I don't know what you're talking about!" he repeated.

I sighed. "Of course you do." I walked in a circle around him, inspecting him. His magical signature wasn't actually all that strong. I frowned and tapped my chin. "Is it because you aren't strong enough to hold all this magic inside you? But you wanted great power so you stole it and stored it here?" I raised the mug. "And now you use it to fuel all the crap you do in this building?"

"It's not crap!"

He hadn't denied what he'd done. Who had the bastard

stolen the magic from? "You turned my friends to stone. I'd say it's crap."

I stuck my finger through the cup's handhold and began to spin it around. Mauritius paled even more.

"So here's the situation," I said. "You tell us what we want to know, or I'll break your cup."

"It won't shatter. It's protected."

"Yes, but my friend here has heavenly fire. I'm pretty sure that will destroy it."

Declan raised his hand. Holy fire flickered around it.

Mauritius squeaked. "But my business…"

"You won't have *any* business if I destroy your magic." I leaned closer. "And I would be *delighted* to."

I had very few friends in this world, and he'd hurt them.

"I'd listen to the lady," Declan said. "She'd do it in a heartbeat. Might as well take the risk of telling us."

Mauritius vibrated with rage. "My staff will be coming soon."

"Maybe." Declan shrugged. "We're not worried about that."

"How do you break the spell that turned my friends to stone?" I demanded. "I'm out of patience."

Mauritius fidgeted, his gaze going from the mug to Declan's still flaming hand. "You can't break the spell."

"What the hell do you mean?" I was going to break the damned mug out of spite.

"Only the person who deployed the orb and cast the spell can break it." He smiled evilly. "A little safeguard I put in place."

Dick. "Who deployed the orb?"

He shut his mouth tight.

I strode toward Declan, holding out the mug so he could grab it with his flaming hand. He reached for it.

Mauritius jerked in Declan's grip. "Wait!"

"Who?"

"An Oraxia demon."

I frowned. "What is that?"

"Don't know everything, do you?" He smirked.

"You're an irritating little worm," I said. "Now tell me, what kind of demon is that?"

He shrugged. "From the Dark World, I think. Some kind of mercenary."

Made sense it would be a demon, since the Council had drafted me for this. "Mercenary? Who was he working for?"

This was the biggest question: *who* would do this, and why?

"I don't know."

Damn it.

I believed him. I didn't want to, but I did. Not only was I good at discerning lies, but he was a bad liar and scared to death on top of that.

"So, only the demon can break the spell. How?"

"There's a disengagement charm he must say. *Just* him. Only his voice will disengage them."

Shit, shit, shit. My friends could be stone forever. And demons were really hard to threaten. They were so violent and goal oriented that they didn't have a normal creature's fear of death. It was why they made great mercenaries.

"Wait..." I frowned. "Did you say, *them*?"

Mauritius snapped his jaw shut.

"How many?" Declan demanded. "How many orbs did you sell him?" He shook Mauritius lightly.

"Six," he choked out.

Oh, quadruple shit. Six?

Declan shook Mauritius again. "What else do we need to know?"

"Nothing!"

"Tell us. I can see it in your eyes."

Mauritius frowned. "If he dies, or all of his orbs are deployed, the spell will be permanent."

Permanent. Just the word made me want to vomit.

My friends' lives were at risk, and we had no idea who was doing this. And the only way to figure it out was to catch the damned demon. He was our only clue.

The sound of footsteps in the hall caught my attention. At least a dozen pairs, some of them belonging to really big people.

My gaze caught on Declan. "Time to go."

The first mage barreled into the room a moment later.

He nodded and let go of Mauritius.

"Hey, Declan," I said. "Catch."

I tossed the coffee mug to him. Instinct made him reach up and grab it with his flaming right hand. The coffee mug incinerated.

Mauritius shrieked, a sound of such rage that the hair on my arms stood up.

I looked at him and grinned like a shark. "That's for being such a bastard."

"You didn't keep your word." He turned hot eyes on us, full of hatred.

"Nope." I only kept my word to Mari. Fuck this guy.

The mage who'd run into the room raised a hand that flamed red, ready to hurl a fireball at us. Four more mages piled into the room after him, their signatures a clashing combination of rotten garlic, burning tires, icy wind, and acidic slime.

There was a door behind Mauritius leading into another part of the building. I sprinted for it, flipping up my hood as I ran.

I glanced back in time to see the fire mage hurl a fireball right at me. At the last second, I darted left, feeling the heat of it against my cheek. Declan dodged a massive icicle that would have pierced his heart.

I sprinted through the door that led to the back room, and Declan followed.

The room was some kind of workshop, full of tables and glass walls that divided it into smaller spaces. All sorts of potion ingredients and tools sat on the tables, with magical charms in various states of creation.

The mages hurtled into the room after us, hurling fireballs, icicles, and sonic booms. The air lit up with magic and color. Declan dived behind one of the glass walls and flipped a heavy table to use as cover.

I sprinted to join him, ducking behind the wooden barricade. All around, the glass walls exploded as the mages pelted them with magic. Glass rained down.

"Where are you?" Declan muttered.

"Two feet to your right."

"We can't transport off this floor. We need to break a window."

"Leave that to me."

"I'll take care of the mages." He popped up from behind the table and shot a small blast of lightning at the closest fire mage. The man lit up like a firecracker.

I sprinted toward the huge wall of windows to my right, drawing my mace as I ran. Magic exploded in the air, fire and ice and lightning. Behind me, Declan took out the mages with his lightning, but more of them were coming.

Mauritius was shrieking in the next room, "Get them! Kill them!"

I neared the window, swinging my mace to work up some speed. Once it was really going, I slammed it into the exterior glass. It shattered, raining out and down onto the sidewalk. I prayed no one was taking an evening stroll.

I turned toward Declan, who was already up and racing toward me. I flipped my hood back so he could see me. His brow relaxed as his eyes caught on me. His wings flared from his back, glinting ebony in the light.

When he reached me, he grabbed me around the waist and swung me up. I clutched him around the neck, and he leapt into the sky, his wings catching on the air and carrying us high.

Bitter wind swept my hair back from my face as we shot upward, away from Mauritius's building. I looked back, catching sight of the mages standing in the broken glass wall. They threw fire and ice at us, but Declan dodged easily.

Soon, we were out of range.

I laughed. "Holy fates, that was a great exit."

Declan grinned, gripping me tightly. I looked at him.

Damn, he was handsome. And smart. And brave. And strong.

Oookay, chill, girl. If I was going to have thoughts like that, I might as well get a pink diary with a lock on it and scrawl them inside. But I'd never had that sort of childhood, and I had no plans to regress.

Anyway, I couldn't trust him. That was the end of things, as far as I was concerned.

I shivered and tucked closer to Declan's heat, enjoying the warmth that welled within me. I could do that without trusting him.

He flew us toward a flat rooftop and landed, setting me down. Up here, the windchill was absolutely freezing, and snow pelted my face.

I dug a transport charm out of my pocket and met his gaze. "You coming?"

He nodded.

I chucked the transport charm to the ground, then stepped into the cloud of sparkling gray dust. The ether sucked me in and spat me out in Magic's Bend, on the street in front of my house.

It was cold here, but compared to Toronto, it was basically balmy. A freaking tropical isle. It was much earlier evening here, with people still on the sidewalks. Ancient-looking street lamps cast a golden glow on the street, and the old Victorian buildings rose three stories high on either side of the street. Their grimy exteriors really gave the place a dark-magic feel, but nothing compared to Mauritius's office tower.

Declan arrived next to me, looking around. "You brought us to your place."

"Got a better idea?"

"Nope." He turned to me. "You destroyed his magic."

"Of course I did. He's a bastard. No way I'm keeping my word to a bastard."

"You seem to have trouble keeping your word." The words weren't nice, but there was no meanness to his tone. He was just honest. And he was right. Last time we'd worked together, I'd made a deal not to kill the demon we were after.

Then I'd totally killed the demon. Duh. "I do keep my word. To my sister."

He nodded. "That's something, at least."

I wasn't going to tell some sad-sack story about our pasts and trying to survive and why we were the way we were. It was true, but it didn't matter. I wasn't looking for pity—fates no—or understanding. I didn't have to prove anything to him.

But...

I still liked him.

I couldn't help it, and I wasn't going to lie to myself. I didn't like that he might have a low opinion of me. Except, I didn't know how to change it.

So I changed the subject instead. "I definitely made an enemy out of Mauritius, but the bastard used his magic for the wrong reasons. And it wasn't even his. He'd stolen it. No wonder he couldn't hold on to his position as Arch Magus."

Declan shrugged and nodded. "Can't say that you're wrong."

"Except now we have a big problem."

"*Six* of those charms."

My skin chilled at the thought. The demon could be deploying them even now. But *where?*

"Why are you hunting him?" I asked.

"Same reason as always. Bounty on his head."

"By who?"

"Can't say."

"Fair enough." We both had our secrets.

"Why are *you* hunting him? You didn't even know what kind of demon it was, so you can't be after his blood."

"The people on Factory Row are my friends." And it was the truth. I'd be hunting him for that reason even if the Council hadn't told me to do it. "Let's work together."

He raised his brow. "How the tables have turned."

A smile tugged at the corner of my mouth. I'd been so resistant to working with him before, but this time... My friends' lives were at risk. There were five more charms out there, possibly already deployed or about to be.

As much as I liked to do things alone... "We're better together. That's how we succeeded back there. And this is too important to go it alone."

"I don't suppose I can trust your word that you won't kill the demon right out from under me, can I?"

"You can try." I shrugged. I didn't want to lie to him. "But no. Once I've interrogated him to figure out who put him up to this, I'm going to try to kill him. You can try to catch him."

"That doesn't work for me."

"Let's agree to disagree, then."

"That's what people say when they're fighting about whether or not dinner was good or a baseball team is the best."

I cracked another smile. "Let's cross that bridge when we come to it?"

"That analogy works better." He frowned, clearly mulling it over.

"What's more important to you? Your bounty, or saving the lives of those people turned to stone?"

He groaned, and I knew I had him.

Because the bounty hunter wanted his money, but not nearly as much as the angel wanted to do the right thing.

I nodded. "Excellent. That's settled. We're working together to catch this bastard."

It was weird for me to do something like this, but it was the right thing. I knew it. I turned toward my house, ready to climb the steps to the front.

"On one condition," he said.

Shit. I turned back to him, frowning. "What's that?"

"Tell me why you tried to make me forget about you."

Double shit. The truth was complicated. I liked him, but I didn't want to get involved with anyone in case they figured out what I was. And that was *not* something I could tell him.

"Well?" he asked.

"Fine. I like you, but I didn't want to get into any kind of relationship or whatever. I'm used to being a loner."

"So the solution was to erase my memory? Not just say 'hey, see ya' later?'"

"I didn't say it was the smartest thing to do."

"You strike me as too smart to do something that dumb. For those reasons at least."

"Let's agree to disagree." I tried out the phrase again, hoping that this time, he would go along with it. "Now, come on. We need to make a plan."

He sighed. "Fine. The mission comes first. But I *am* going to figure out what's up with you."

"What's up with me is that I want some food and to make a plan before shit hits the fan and this gets messy."

"I'd say we're already there."

Unfortunately, he was probably right. I climbed the stairs to my house and let myself in. Declan followed behind, and I beelined for my kitchen. Normally, my all-white space would soothe me.

Today, all I could think about was Declan walking right behind me. I could feel his gaze on me, and it warmed me from the inside out. I strode into the kitchen and rang the little bell that connected to the Chinese restaurant down the street. Two rings for two portions, with an extra quick jingle at the end to indicate that I was in a hurry and didn't care what they sent. Normally they'd send me something off of my preferred list, but in situations like this, I wasn't picky.

"Food should be here any minute," I said. The bell was connected to a portal, so it wouldn't take them long at all.

"Chinese?"

"Yes. We can eat on the way to the Order of the Magica offices and tell them to evacuate the city. We don't know where the Oraxia demon will hit next, so best to be prepared." I hated going to the Order—I didn't trust them as far as I could throw them—but we'd be going to a branch of their offices that weren't a threat to me.

"Good plan. Though a lot of people won't listen. We don't even know if the demon will deploy another orb here."

He had a point, both about the bomb and the people who wouldn't listen. Folks in Magic's Bend were stubborn, especially Darklaners. A while ago, our whole town had almost been sucked into a portal and destroyed, and most of Darklane had stayed put.

The food appeared on the carton, and I handed one to Declan without looking inside. "Chopsticks?"

He nodded, and I handed him one of the paper packets of disposable wooden utensils.

I dug into mine as we left the kitchen. I was so hungry that it tasted like heaven. We'd only been here a couple minutes, fortunately, but we still needed to get a move on. "Let's go. We'll hit up Order headquarters first."

I *really* hoped the government would listen to me. What kind of story was I going to feed them about how I'd come upon this information, though? The truth worked, for the most part. Except for the fact that it didn't answer the question of why a blood sorceress like me was on the hunt.

For my friends.

I'd eaten almost half my lo mein by the time we reached the foyer and the alarm went off. It blared loud and fierce, with red smoke forming at the ceiling.

"What's that?" Declan asked.

I opened the door to the outside and shoved him onto the front step.

"I need you to wait here." I pressed a hand to his chest. "Don't leave this spot."

He frowned at me. "What's going on?"

"It's like a phone call, and I have to go answer it. It'll only take a minute."

He gave me a skeptical look, and I tried to smile in a way that said, "Trust me."

Finally, he nodded, though I didn't think he'd bought the message I was trying to sell with my smile. But I didn't have a choice. I needed to answer this call.

I shut the door in his face, locked it, then raced back to my workshop. Without Mari, I'd have to move the table on my own. I set my carton of lo mein on the fireplace mantel and sliced my finger, dripping blood onto one corner of the table, then walked to the other corner and pressed my hand to it.

As usual, the table levitated and drifted to the side, but I could feel the strain. It really helped to have Mari use her magic, too.

I walked toward the invisible trapdoor and fed it two drops of blood. When the ground disappeared, I raced down the spiral stone staircase, letting the cool air of the earth envelop me. I passed the aerlig vines and the Lights of Truth and reached the bottom of the stairs in record time. I hurried toward the glittering blue pool and kicked off my shoes before stepping into the water.

I chanted, "Here I be, let me see."

Agatha appeared almost immediately, her ghostly form nearly transparent. "There's been another attack."

"Shit."

"Government Lane."

"Double shit."

"Language."

"That's what you're concerned about?"

She tsked.

"Do you know anything about Oraxia demons?" I asked.

She frowned. "No one has seen an Oraxia demon in centuries."

"What can you tell me about them?"

"Not much, unfortunately. They're very strong and very loyal. Perhaps the most loyal demon there is."

"Loyal to whom? Those who hire them?"

She nodded. "Most demons have some loyalty to those who get them out of the underworld or the Dark World, but Oraxia demons were known to be particularly dedicated. They'll complete whatever task they were chosen for."

Damn. Most demons could only get out of the underworld if someone on earth helped them do it. In exchange, the demon was normally required to work for that person as a mercenary.

Their loyalty could often be swayed, though. But not the Oraxia demon, apparently.

Just our luck. "Anything else I should know?"

"Just that you need to hurry."

"Isn't that always the way?" I gave her a small smile. "Thanks, Agatha. Wish me luck. My friends' lives are on the line."

She gave a small nod, which was the most I was going to get out of her. Agatha wasn't big on emotion.

Quickly, I pressed my fingertips to my comms charm. "Mari?"

"Yeah? You okay?"

"I'm fine. But don't come back to Magic's Bend."

"What? Why?" Panic flared in her voice.

"More orbs are out there. A second one just went off on Government Lane."

"Shit."

"Exactly. So don't come back into the city limits. We don't know where the next one will go off."

"What about you?"

"That's why you need to stay out. Someone will have to rescue me." I could just imagine her scowl. "Any luck with Claire?"

"Just found her. She's fine."

My shoulders relaxed. Thank fates for small favors. "I'm going to go check out Government Lane. Then we can meet and make a plan."

"Where do you want to meet?"

"Somewhere right outside of town. I don't think he'll deploy one where there aren't any people. What's the point?"

"How about the beach to the north?"

It was one of our favorite places, a quiet stretch of rocks and driftwood that butted up against the wild Pacific Ocean. "Okay, see you there. Safe hunting."

"Safe hunting."

I cut the magic in the comms charm and hurried back up the stairs, spiraling my way toward the surface. When I reached the aerlig vines, I caught sight of a figure trapped within them. The vines twisted around the huge form of a man.

Declan.

Damn it.

5

I stopped in front of the mass of vines, staring hard at Declan's trapped form. "Fancy seeing you here."

"What the hell is this place?" His voice was muffled behind the vine that partially covered his mouth.

"My secret lair. I locked you out on the front step. What the hell are you doing?"

"Trying to break into your secret lair and figure out what the hell is going on with you."

"So you broke into my house?" I added some extra chill to my voice.

"You need a better lock and protection charm."

Any chill that I had evaporated. "It's one of the best!"

Damn it. Besides the lock on the door and the protection charm that he'd apparently managed to break through, I'd trusted him to stay where I told him to stay because he was an angel.

A *fallen* angel.

I was an idiot. Declan was a mix of good and bad, like I was. In fact, he was way too much like me. Which was exactly why I shouldn't trust him.

Mari and I didn't trust anyone except each other, and he wasn't doing a great job of convincing me to do otherwise.

I pressed my hand to the vines that bound him. I could just barely get a hint of Declan's intentions through the vines that had stopped him. They stopped anyone who didn't have permission or who had ill intentions. Declan didn't have ill intentions according to the vines—which I could trust—but he also didn't have permission to be here, so they'd wrapped him up.

"Thanks, guys," I murmured.

"You're talking to the plant?"

"Yep." I used my mind to command the plants to let him go.

Slowly they unwound, freeing Declan. I pointed up the stairs. "We're going that way."

"What the hell is down that way?" He pointed down the stairs.

"None of your business."

"That just makes it more interesting."

"My shoe collection, all right?"

"No."

"Weapons."

"More believable, at least." He turned and started up the stairs. "I'm going to get to the bottom of you, though. Mystery wrapped in an enigma wrapped in a riddle."

I'd joked with him about that before, and he remembered. "No you won't."

He chuckled, as if the idea were absurd. I followed him up to the room and put the table back in place, then grabbed my carton of lo mein off the mantel. I'd lost my appetite when Agatha had told me about Government Lane, but I knew from experience that if I didn't eat, I'd weaken.

"Let's go." I shoved a bite in my mouth, not bothering to tell Declan about Government Lane. We'd see it soon enough, and I didn't want him knowing I had an inside track on what was going on. That would invite way too many questions.

I finished my food as we hurried out of the house and around the corner to the alley where I'd parked my car. It was an old white Cadillac, a total boat of a car, and I loved it. Maybe it was a weird choice, but it was mine.

I tossed my empty carton a trash bin, then climbed behind the wheel. Declan got in the passenger seat. A tingle of fear streaked down my spine at the thought of the demon who was out there, deploying the rest of the orbs in Magic's Bend. Two down, four to go.

At any moment, he could deploy one right near me, and I'd turn to stone. I swallowed hard. It was like a horrible game of Russian roulette.

It wouldn't take long to reach Government Lane, which was near the Business District. Anxiety tugged at me, and I drew a bag of Cheetos from the ether. My emergency stash. I crunched on them while I drove, offering Declan some. He declined.

"You're missing out." Not only did they taste good, they helped minimize feelings of stress. I was pretty sure it even said that on the bag.

I polished them off and turned onto the main street in Government Lane. The big marble buildings looked very official and administrative. There weren't any gawkers there yet. Partially because it was nighttime and this part of town was closed down. And partially because the detection devices that would pick up on the deployment of dark magic were located *in* Government Lane. The orb had probably frozen them, along with the people who would answer the distress call.

This was bad freaking news.

Even worse news was the fact that many government officials lived in swanky apartments on this street so they were close to work. The Oraxia demon had effectively taken out our government in one fell swoop.

I kept my mouth shut about it, though, and turned toward an open parking spot along the street.

"We should go to the mayor's house," Declan said. "Tell him first, then he can get the word out for people to evacuate."

"Good plan." I turned the car off and climbed out.

The mayor would probably be frozen, but no way would I mention that. Then I'd have to explain how I knew.

I pressed my lips together and hurried to the big townhouse that belonged to the mayor. It was built of white marble with columns in front, and I'd always found it to be quite gaudy. I climbed the stairs and banged on the door, waiting.

Declan waited next to me, his frown growing as the seconds ticked on.

"Even if the mayor isn't home, his staff would be." Declan turned around to inspect the street. "Oddly quiet here."

"It's off hours."

"Still."

"You think something is wrong."

"I feel it. Don't you?"

I shivered, finally nodding. "Yeah. Let's break in."

"A woman after my own heart."

He pulled a little packet of tiny lock-picking tools from his pocket and got to work. We were inside in less than a minute.

I stepped into the quiet foyer. The lights still flickered, and I could hear the faint sound of a TV coming from the left.

"That's not good." Quietly, I moved toward the TV. When I caught sight of the mayor's frozen form, sitting in an armchair in front of the screen, my shoulders slumped.

I'd believed Agatha when she'd told me the orb had been deployed here, but I hated seeing it.

"Damn it." Declan strode toward the mayor and crouched down to inspect him. "He already deployed a second orb."

"Recently, I think. The mayor probably just sat down to watch the eight o'clock news." I looked at the clock over the mantel. Eight thirty. The bomb had gone off before we'd even returned to Magic's Bend. "If we assume that, then there was about a six-hour gap between orbs."

"That doesn't give us a lot of time." He walked to the window and looked out. "The whole neighborhood is frozen. Just like Factory Row."

"That's probably the range of the orb. And there are six major neighborhoods in Magic's Bend. Factory Row, Government Lane, the Business District, Darklane, the Historic District, and the Museum & Academic Area."

"So he's probably planning to freeze the whole city. And the gap in time it takes to deploy the orbs may be him regaining his magic after he uses it to deploy the orbs."

The theories were sound. "Let's get out of here. My sister is nearly back from her trip, and I want to meet her on the outskirts."

"Good. We could use more help."

I pressed my fingertips to my comms charm and called Mari again. I wanted Declan to see me make these plans so he didn't realize I'd *already* made them. "Mari?"

"Yeah?"

"We'll meet you in fifteen at the beach north of town. Can you make it by then?"

"Sure." Her voice indicated that she thought the second call was a bit weird, but she'd never mention it unless she could see and confirm that I was alone. I cut the contact and looked at Declan. "Let's go."

The drive to the beach was quick, with minimal traffic. Considering that about thirty percent of the population had turned to stone, I wasn't surprised. I parked in my usual spot under the big tree and climbed out, sucking in the fresh ocean breeze. I loved it here. Always had. When we'd first escaped Grimrealm, I'd spent a lot of time swimming here, not caring how cold it was.

Declan climbed out, and we hurried to the shore, spotting two figures sitting on a big log and looking out to sea. Claire spotted me and stood. I hurried up to her and flung my arms around her.

I pulled back, suddenly feeling awkward, and met her surprised gaze. I'd never had a hugging relationship with anyone except Mari, but I'd been so worried about her.

I cleared my throat. "Thank fates you're safe."

"I missed it by only a few minutes, I think." She pulled back from me. "Nothing was strange when I left. But you saw Connor."

"Yes. But don't worry. We'll save him. And the FireSouls."

She nodded, worry clouding her eyes.

"What's the status?" Mari asked, careful not to mention that she already knew Government Lane was down.

I explained what we'd seen.

Claire and Mari's faces paled as I explained our theory about six-hour gaps between orb deployments, and how little we knew about Oraxia demons.

"We need to evacuate the city," Mari said.

"It's going to be hard without the government backing us up," Claire said.

"At least there is physical proof that the threat is real and spreading," Declan said.

It was dark, but true.

"A lot of people will leave," I said. "Darklaners won't, and a scattering of others."

"We'll get on it," Mari said. "Claire and I can go door to door. We'll make sure people evacuate."

It wasn't a permanent solution, but we needed whatever Band-Aids we could manage right now.

"Be sure you stay out of Magic's Bend while you hunt the Oraxia demon," Claire said. "If you need to come back in, tell us so we can leave."

We were all highly conscious of the fact that at least one of us needed to stay outside of Magic's Bend at all times. Just in case.

"I think we need to go to the Undercover Protectorate," I said. "Someone else needs to know about this."

Mari nodded. "I'd trust them more than the Order of the Magica."

We could go to the main branch of the Order and seek help there—they were probably already aware of the problem—but as we'd seen back on Factory Row, they were slow and cowardly about addressing it. The lives of their investigators were more important than those of the innocent citizens of Magic's Bend.

Whereas the Undercover Protectorate was a private organization dedicated to protecting those who needed it.

Right now, Magic's Bend qualified.

And we had friends there. *And* they had a miraculous library that might contain info about the Oraxia demon. Multiple birds with one stone and all that.

"Okay. Good plan." I looked at Mari. "Can you give us a ride to Scotland?"

"Be happy to."

I gave Claire another quick hug. "Be careful."

She nodded. "You too."

Mari held out her hands, and we took them. A moment later, the ether sucked us in and spun us through space, making my stomach pitch. Finally, it spit us out in the dusky light of a Highland morning.

The Undercover Protectorate was located in the middle of nowhere, their operations run out of an enormous old castle with a huge wall surrounding it. We stood at the front gate, a huge wooden thing that was enforced against most types of magical attacks.

"Safe hunting." Mari squeezed me tight, then nodded at Declan.

He nodded back.

"Safe hunting." I smiled at her, then she disappeared.

I turned to the castle gate. "Hey! Open up!"

A moment later, a head stuck out over the edge of the ramparts. Long dark hair blew in the breeze, and the woman smiled. "Aerdeca! Long time, no see."

"Hey, Bree. Can we come in?"

"Yeah, of course."

Slowly, the gate rose.

"This place hardly seems like it's from this century," Declan said.

"Never been here before?"

"Never even heard of it."

"Well, you're in for a treat."

As the gate rose higher, Bree appeared, a coffee cup steaming in her hand. She was tall and pale, with long dark hair and a big smile. She was a Dragon God and the only living Valkyrie.

"It's your lucky day. I just came out for an early walk." Her gaze moved over my clothes, and she frowned. "What's wrong? You're wearing your fight clothes."

She only ever saw me in these when we were about to head into battle. "Magic's Bend needs help."

Bree's brows rose. "The whole place?"

"The whole place." I gestured to Declan. "This is Declan O'Shea, bounty hunter and fallen angel."

He stuck out his hand and they shook.

Bree looked back to me. "I'll call everyone to the Round Room."

"Thank you." The Round Room was their version of a war room, and damned if we didn't need to plan an attack.

She pressed her finger to the comms charm that hung around her neck and spoke to someone as we walked up toward the massive castle in the middle of the lawn.

The massive stone structure rose tall, with turrets and towers added here and there. Dozens of windows glittered with light, making the place look as inviting as I knew it to be. The grounds were enormous, containing stables on one side, a forest, a stone circle, and a cliff that plunged right into the sea.

We reached the big stairs and climbed up toward the huge wooden doors. They swung open to admit us to the entrance hall, a big space with a soaring ceiling and a sweeping staircase leading to the higher levels. The scent of breakfast from the kitchens wafted up, bacon and coffee.

People were streaming up from the door that led down to the kitchen that was located on the bottom floor, cups of coffee and sandwiches in their hands as they ran to the Round Room.

"Come on. Everyone will be there soon." Bree led us up the stairs and down a wide hallway.

Three cats sprinted by, headed in the opposite direction. The big white one—Princess Snowflake III, I'd heard her called once —had a jeweled bracelet clutched in her teeth. A skinny black cat with wings followed close behind, with the rear brought up by an orange one.

A blonde woman joined us as we walked. As usual, we didn't hug in greeting. In the past, I'd seen that Ana was a hugger, but I wasn't. Not when I was Aerdeca, at least.

"Hello, Ana." I pointed to Declan and made introductions.

Ana smiled and stuck her hand out. She was Bree's sister. Also a Dragon God, and a Druid. DragonGods were a crazy powerful combo of dragon magic and godly magic, and each one represented a mythical pantheon. Bree was Viking, Ana Druid, and their sister Rowan was Greek.

"Rowan's out on a job," Ana said, as if she could read my mind. Her gaze moved over my clothes, worry creasing her brow, just like it had her sister's. "What's wrong? Why aren't you wearing your nice clothes?"

Everyone was apparently very attuned to the two sides of my personality. Silk equaled business as usual. Fight clothes equaled trouble.

"Magic's Bend needs help, or everyone will die."

"Shit."

We filtered into the Round Room, which was exactly what it sounded like. A circular room in one of the big towers. A huge round table dominated the space. Tapestries and torches covered the walls. Jude, the leader of the Protectorate, already sat at the table, surrounded by the other department heads. She was a beautiful dark-skinned woman with braids and blue eyes that sparkled with starlight.

"Aerdeca." She nodded at me. "It's been a while."

"I know." I gestured to Declan and introduced him. We sat, joining the approximately twenty people at the table. Mostly department heads and anyone who was on staff who wasn't out on a job, I had to assume. They took all problems seriously.

"I can assume this isn't a friendly visit? Since you never actually visit, that is."

While I liked everyone at the Protectorate, she was right. I didn't visit just to shoot the shit. Not my style. I showed up if they needed help, but that was it. And now I was here to get a return on the favors I'd accrued over the years.

"We have a serious problem in Magic's Bend." I explained the orbs, the Oraxia demon, and the fact that our government was now frozen, too.

Jude frowned. "The Order will move too slowly on this, it sounds like."

"Exactly. Mordaca is evacuating the town, but she needs help."

"And we need to figure out how to repair the damage done by the orbs," Declan said.

"We can send people to help Mordaca evacuate the town. And our resources are yours."

"We need to figure out how to compel the demon to undo the spells," Declan said. "He's the only one who can do it."

"Then it sounds like you need to learn more about an Oraxia demon. Our library may be able to help you there."

"I can try to find the demon," Ana said. "Though no promises that my Druid sense can manage it."

Ana had an usual type of seer power gifted to her by the Celtic gods that helped her find answers to her questions.

I smiled at her. "Thank you. Time is everything."

She nodded.

"That's settled, then," Jude said. "We'll deploy a team to Magic's Bend to perform evacuations. Ana will try to find the demon. And you, Aerdeca and Declan, are welcome to our library or any resources that we have here."

"Thank you." I stood, ready to get to work.

Ana darted out of the room without another word, Bree on her heels.

Jude led us to the library. We walked through hallways that had been built during various periods in the castle's history. Ancient stone corridors and beautifully wallpapered passages with gleaming wooden floors all competed to be the most beautiful.

Jude pushed open the door. "Florian will help you. I'm off to rally the troops."

"Thank you, Jude."

"You've helped us many times. We're happy to return the favor." She smiled. "Anyway, it's our job."

She turned and left, and I stepped into the library. The ceiling soared high overhead, the tall walls covered with bookshelves that were stuffed full to the brim with colorful leather books. Paintings hung over some of them, giving the room a cozy and cluttered feel. Fireplaces were built into each wall, roaring with warmth. Big chairs and heavy wooden tables filled the space.

In front of the fire sat a dog bed. Three ghostly forms filled it. The Pugs of Destruction. One had horns, one had wings, and one had fangs. All were trouble.

Declan craned his head back, inspecting the space with wide eyes. "Where do we even start?"

A ghostly blue form drifted through the wall at the back. The figure wore clothing from the eighteenth century, if I had to guess, with a ruffled cravat and a curly wig atop his head.

He floated up to us and dropped into a deep bow. "Florian Bumbledomber, at your service." He looked up. "Aerdeca. Declan."

I'd met the ghost briefly once, but never actually visited him in his library. I pointed to Declan. "How did you know his name?"

"I spied on the meeting in the Round Room." He gave a cheeky grin. "Which means I know just what you are looking for. Wait here."

"Well, that's convenient," Declan said.

"No kidding."

We sat at a table while the pugs continued to snore in their beds. The air shimmered next to me on the table, and Wally appeared.

Declan jumped slightly, startled.

"Hey, Wally." I smiled at the cat.

I like this place.

"Me too."

"Are you talking to the cat?" Declan asked.

"Yep."

"Can he talk back?"

"Yep. To me, at least. I think it's some kind of telepathy." I looked at Wally. "What are you doing here?"

Felt you leave the city. Wanted to see where you went.

"Cool. We're hunting an Oraxia demon."

Wally narrowed his flame-red eyes, smoke flickering around him. *Sounds familiar.* He shrugged a little shoulder. *Don't remember why.*

A few moments later, Florian drifted out from behind the bookshelves, a small book clutched in his hands.

Damn. That thing was little.

He nodded at Wally. "Greetings, friend." He tilted his head toward the Pugs of Destruction, who continued to snore at the fire. "Don't terrorize the dogs."

Wally's head moved back, an offended-looking motion. *I would never.*

"Well, the other cats would."

"You can hear him?" I asked Florian.

"Ghosts can usually communicate with animals. He held up the little book, and a frown creased his ghostly face. "I'm afraid there isn't very much about the Oraxia demons."

I wasn't surprised, but I couldn't help the disappointment. "We'll take whatever you've got."

He set the book on the table. It was tiny and gray, clearly not a book from this room. There had to be more to the library that I didn't know about. Another section, maybe. But I trusted Florian to give me all the info he had.

"You'll want to flip to page twenty-four," he said.

I did as he instructed, peering at the tiny print. "Whoa. Oraxia demons were *created*. Like, built by a mad scientist. It says that a figure named the Devyver created them. He lives in the Shade City of Dark World."

Wally blinked red eyes. *That's why I remember. That place is terrible. Oraxia demons do come from there.*

"It's definitely a start," Declan said.

"Thank you, Florian." I held out the book to him.

The ghost smiled and took the book back.

I turned to Declan. "We need a plan."

"We need to find the demon's weakness. Or find a way to compel it. The only way to succeed is by breaking its loyalty to its masters and forcing it to say the counterspell."

I swallowed hard. "So we need to go to the Dark World."

6

I *can take you to Dark World.*

I looked up at Wally, surprised. "You can?"

Hellcat, remember? Going to hell is kind of my thing.

"But this is a little different than the underworld." Which was full of demons, but also the souls of humans. The Dark World was just demon territory, the darkest and most horrible place in existence, as far as I'd ever heard. Besides maybe the DMV.

Doesn't matter. I can go. Went once. Not a fan. His whiskers quivered, as if in distaste.

"Thanks." I turned to Declan. "Looks like we have a ride."

"A ride where?" A feminine voice drifted over from the door.

I turned to see Hedy, the pretty, lavender-haired witch who was the head of research and development at the Protectorate. She wore a loose dress with colorful skirts and looked a bit like a hippie. I hadn't spoken to her much in the past, but I knew who she was. She'd been at the meeting, so Declan had briefly met her as well.

"Hi, Hedy," I said.

"I brought you some Power-Up Potion." She held out two

vials. "When I heard what you're up against, I realized you'd probably be working around the clock. I'd save these until you really need them, but they'll give you another day's worth of energy when you do."

"Oh, thanks." I smiled. That really would come in handy. I took the potions.

Who's she?

I looked at Wally. "That's Hedy, one of the strongest witches here." I looked at Hedy. "Meet Wally, my...friend."

'My cat' suggested ownership, and frankly, Wally did whatever the hell he wanted. He couldn't be owned.

Ask her for a potion to make you look like a demon. You'll need to blend in down there.

"Thanks." I turned to Hedy and made the request, explaining our circumstances.

She rubbed her chin and thought, her eyes going distant. "Yes. I think I can get you something that will work." She eyed my white ghost suit. "And you're going to need new clothes."

Fortunately, it didn't take her long to get us two potions from her laboratory, which was located in a small building away from the main castle.

"So I don't blow the whole place up," she'd said. "Just a little security measure."

We'd also needed potions that would amplify the little bit of dark magic that each of us possessed. Even if we looked like demons, our signatures could give us away if we weren't careful. So could my white clothes, which would look strange if the rest of me looked like a demon. Maybe there was a demon out there who dressed all in pristine white, but it was unlikely and it'd make me stand out like an elephant at the symphony. Bree had loaned me some black fight wear, and I'd stashed my ghost suit in the ether, a handy—if expensive—spell.

Now we had the potions we needed, along with sandwiches from the castle cook, Hans, and we stood on the yard.

I swallowed a bite of sandwich and looked at Wally, who stood at my feet, his smoky black form wavering in the wind. "So, what's the drill here?"

I will take us to the train station in Dark World. Then we will go to Shade City and find this Devyver.

"Train station?"

Dark World is not like you would expect. And the demons won't like you, so don't let them know what you are.

"Deal." I finished off my sandwich and looked at Declan. He'd also finished his. "Ready to take these potions and go?"

He nodded, uncorking the little vial. I did the same, swigging back the dark liquid and nearly gagging. Oh fates, that was *bad*. It tasted like a gym sock smelled, and my eyes watered.

Declan choked. "Oh, that's nasty."

Magic sparked along my arms and legs, a strange tingle that made me shiver. I inspected Declan for any changes. His form wavered, and I caught a glimpse of a spectral demon form overlaying his normal body. The demon was a hulking creature with dark gray-and-white mottled skin, huge horns, and claws as long as my fingers.

Hedy had tried to make us look like a species that happened to possess some of our natural magic, so we could fight but still stay in character. He was a lightning demon. I was some random species, though, since I didn't do anything obvious like throw fire or ice.

"Your form is flickering," Declan said.

"Hedy said that might happen." Declan and I would be able to partially see through the enchantments, but the demons should only see our demon forms. I looked down at Wally. "Do we look like demons?"

Yes. You're ugly as a dog's arse.

"That's good enough for me." I looked at Declan. "Hellcat says we're good."

The disguises would only work for twelve hours, which was fine, since we didn't have that much time anyway. We were going to need to be quick about this. We both took the second potion —the one that would amplify our dark magic signatures so we'd actually feel like demons as well as look like them.

Okay, get ready. Wally twisted himself around our ankles, weaving in and out like a cat who wanted a scratch. It looked entirely normal, except for the smoke that drifted up from his body, enveloping us. It didn't choke me like normal smoke would, though it did prickle against my skin. Soon, the day was entirely blacked out, and the ether began to tug at me.

I reached for Declan's hand and gripped it tight.

The ether sucked us in, pulling us through space. It was a rough ride—way more so than normal. When it spat me out in a place that smelled of sulfur and rotten fish, my head was whirling. I gasped, trying to catch my breath.

There was a heaviness to the air here, a misery and dread that floated on the wind.

All around, activity heaved. Dozens of demons of all different species filled the antique-looking train station. It was a lot like Darklane—Victorian styling overlaid by a layer of grime, the natural byproduct of dark magic. There was a row of ticket booths on one side, each manned by an angry-looking demon.

It was almost surreal to see a demon doing a normal job, rather than hunting and killing.

Then a demon in the closest booth shot a bolt of flame at the customer standing right in front of him, lighting his hair on fire. The demon in the booth growled, "Don't try to cheat me."

Okay, so not *that* normal.

Demon normal.

Across from the booths, there were six train tracks, three of which had old-fashioned steam trains pulled up to them. The station was open to the sky, which was filled with heavy gray clouds.

I shivered at the ominous feeling in the air and looked down at Wally. "Now what?"

No one paid attention to the hellcat, fortunately, and everyone ignored us as well.

We need money to buy a ticket to Shade City. Demon money.

I looked up at Declan. "Ready to rob someone?"

He nodded.

It was the only way to get the cash we needed, and I didn't feel even a tiny bit bad about stealing from a demon. The magic in the air here was so disgusting that it made it clear all of these demons were evil. That's what made a demon into a demon— evil intentions and a willingness to casually hurt others.

In the question of what came first, the demon or the evil, the answer was always the evil. Half demons—*extremely* rare— could be good since they had something else in them to moderate the evil side. But the figures surrounding us were all full-blooded.

I scouted the area, looking for a quiet spot and a smaller demon. Near the end of the booths, there was a series of shops. There were probably dark alleys behind.

"This way." I gestured for Declan to follow, and we cut through the crowd, headed toward the shops.

As we passed the booth that sold tickets to Shade City, I checked out the prices. Ten durkas.

"Durkas must be a demon dollar," Declan murmured.

I nodded, continuing on.

As we neared the shops, I nearly gagged at what I saw inside the windows. One was full of demon heads on spikes. I didn't bother looking in the rest. We made our way to the side of the shops and found a dark alley.

To my delight, a demon about my size walked by. He was skinny, dressed entirely in black leather, and had his horns filed into super sharp points. His magic reeked of rotten cabbage and felt like slime under my fingernails.

As soon as he'd passed us, Declan and I jumped on him and dragged him back into the alley. Declan clamped a hand over his mouth, and once we were in the darkened area, he knocked the demon on the head so hard that he slumped over, passed out.

He laid him on the ground, and I rifled through his pockets and pulled out a bag of weird black coins. I dumped them into my palm and then held them out to Wally. "Are these durkas?"

Yes.

"Great." I counted out eight coins marked with a 10. That was enough for a round-trip ticket for each of us, just in case, and a bit extra for bribes. I stuffed the pouch back into the demon's pocket.

"He'll be out for a while." Declan dragged the demon's body to the wall and propped it up so he looked like a passed-out drunk.

"Cool. Let's get on the train."

We walked to the ticket booth, and I looked down at Wally. "Do I need to buy you a ticket?"

I don't know. I'll stay out of sight.

"Cool." We stopped in front of the ticket booth, and I eyed the clerk, trying to look mean and tough, all while praying that my demon illusion was holding up.

The demon selling tickets was some kind of ice demon, from the look of his pale blue skin, and if he got pissed, I'd need to be fast.

"Two to Shade City," I growled.

The demon hesitated slightly, studying us. My heart jumped into my throat, and I was careful to control my breathing and look relaxed. Finally, the demon shrugged and took the money, handing us two tickets.

I could feel his stare on us as we walked away, and the hair at the back of my neck stood up.

"I don't think our disguises are that great," I murmured to Declan.

"Could be our magic. Even with the amplification, you don't smell nearly as bad as these guys."

Amplifying our dark magic had worked to help us sneak through Grimrealm, but that place wasn't nearly as bad as this one.

I avoided eye contact as I slipped through the crowd, hurrying toward the platform that was marked with the words *Shade City*. The train's engine belched black smoke as we neared, and the once red paint job was thoroughly coated in grime. Even the windows were almost entirely blacked out from it.

We found the compartment written on the tickets—it had only two seats, thank fates—and sat down. Wally appeared a moment later, sitting on the floor.

His whiskers twitched. *It's small.*

"I don't think anything here is going to be very nice."

And it stinks.

"You like the finer things in life, huh?"

I know I like sitting in your bathroom sink and eating souls, so if those are the finer things, then yes.

"Fair enough." I looked out the window. Someone had wiped the grime off the middle of it, and I could watch the demons outside. Unlike a human train station, there were no demon children. Demons didn't actually have childhoods, since there was an element of innocence to that. And there was nothing innocent about evil personified. Like Athena had popped out of Zeus's forehead fully formed, demons entered the world as adults. They were created when enough dark magic coalesced in one place and was struck by a huge amount of energy, like from lightning or a tidal wave.

Declan shut the sliding door that closed off our compartment, and I relaxed. "This is more sophisticated than I expected."

"Evil doesn't mean stupid," Declan said.

"Good point."

The steam whistle blew, a piercing sound that made me wince, and the train started to rumble along. The vibration was almost soothing, and Wally settled down on the floor with a satisfied look in his flame-red eyes.

Soon, we'd left the train station behind and were powering through a deserted wasteland cut through with massive chasms. The ground looked like it had been in constant motion in the past, splitting and cracking as giants walked over it. Lightning struck in the distance, the dark clouds swirling faster than I'd ever seen them move on earth.

"Does anything live out there?" I asked Wally.

I don't know.

"How long is the ride?"

Don't know that either. Not good with time.

"Two hours," Declan said. "Saw it on the board."

"Thanks. I was distracted by the demon."

Declan nodded.

Despite the stench of dark magic and the terrifying landscape out the window, the rumble of the train soothed me. I was exhausted. Not tired enough to take the potion, but the day was starting to catch up to me.

I yawned and tried to lean my head against the window, but it was so grimy that I gave up almost immediately.

"Lean on me," Declan said.

I frowned, tempted. I was beat, and I really wouldn't mind touching him. Except, that violated my newly made hands-off policy.

"I won't bite. Promise."

I caught sight of the smile on Declan's face, and fortunately, it was during one of the moments when he looked like himself instead of a demon.

Sleep. I'll keep watch.

"Thanks, Wally." I looked at Declan. "He said he'd keep a lookout if we both took a nap."

"I'm not sure I'm keen on lowering my guard in Dark World."

"Wally can be trusted. And anyway, it's less safe to be tired on a mission like this. And we should save those Power-Up Potions until we really need them." Who knew how long this could possibly take? "But anyway, up to you."

I leaned my head against his shoulder and closed my eyes. The warm heat of his muscles felt like the only nice thing in this world, and I focused on that. Finally, Declan relaxed.

Sleep caught me hard in its grip, a nightmare close on its tail.

The cold cell was just like the one back in Grimrealm. I shivered on the cold stone, my mind spinning. We'd only been out for a year, and already we were back under the thumb of someone else who wanted to use us. The Council of Demon Slayers had helped us escape our evil aunt and uncle, but we'd almost immediately gotten ourselves into trouble again.

We'd had one glorious year of freedom in the real world, learning to be demon slayers and finding a life for ourselves in Magic's Bend.

And then we'd trusted Dani. We'd thought she was our friend— the third sister we'd never had. We'd even told her we had Dragon Blood.

It had been the stupidest thing we'd ever done.

Almost immediately, she'd sold us out to the Order of the Magica.

For what, I didn't know. But they'd found us and thrown us in this cell.

And now Mari was being forced to create new magic.

I could see her in the cell across the hall. Iron bars separated us, making it easy for us to see and talk to each other.

Just like Aunt, these bastards had figured out that we would do as they commanded if they threatened the other.

"Mari," I whispered. "Stop."

She didn't even twitch. Mari knelt on the stone floor, her shoulders bowed as black blood poured from her wrists. They were forcing her to create permanent magic. Not the one-and-done little stuff that was created with a drop. The real, lasting magic that came when you poured out more blood than it seemed like your body should hold.

More blood equaled more magic.

I crawled toward the iron bars, weak and exhausted. I had to get to Mari. Somehow, I had to get through these bars.

Her magic began to flow from her, filling the cells. It tasted of whiskey, a burn on the back of my throat. I should be too young to know what that tasted like.

I wasn't too young for anything. Not after the life I'd lived.

Pouring out your magic was the second part of the process. If she survived, she'd wake with new magic.

Tears flowed down my face. "Mari!" I shook the cell bars. "Mari!"

Through the haze of dreams, I felt a warm weight settle on my lap.

Wake up!

Wally's voice finally pierced my woozy consciousness. I sat upright, gasping. Wally sat on my thighs, his concerned red eyes glued to my face.

Are you all right?

Declan was still asleep next to me.

I swallowed and rubbed my face, nodding. "Fine."

Nightmare?

"Yes." I hadn't dreamed of that time in ages. In fact, I'd done my best to force the memories from my mind.

Dani had been our first friend in the real world, and we'd been stupid enough to trust her. She'd almost immediately screwed us. We'd have died if we hadn't escaped. We'd have died later if we hadn't blown the whole experimental magical laboratory to smithereens.

From what Mari and I had been able to piece together, we'd been captured by a rogue operation, a secret branch of the Order of the Magica, meant to find strange supernaturals and use them. Because we'd destroyed the lab—and everyone involved in the operation—we'd been able to disappear.

The remaining members of Order didn't know what we were. Who we were. Theoretically, they weren't all bad. That had been a rogue operation, after all.

Still, I didn't trust the Order as far as I could throw them. They'd used us once; they could use us again.

Hence, the reason for our secrecy.

Tell no one.

We'd agreed it was the only way to stay safe. I squeezed my eyes shut and shook my head.

We're there.

I sucked in a deep breath and nudged Declan. He woke and became alert within a fraction of a second.

I looked out the window, catching sight of the last of the broken plains and the beginnings of Shade City. The buildings themselves were ramshackle, some fifteen or twenty stories high. Many didn't even have walls, looking like they'd been blown out in some apocalyptic event in the past.

The ground was broken asphalt with patches of dirt, and the shop windows were full of terrible stuff, just like they had been at the train station. Demons walked along the streets and sidewalks—there were no cars—and the thing that struck me the most about them was that they looked *bored*. A little worried, too, perhaps. But bored.

There was no one for them to terrify and torture, I guessed. They probably turned on each other, but everyone knew that demons preferred human and Magica targets. It was why they were so keen to get out of Dark World and would act as mercenaries on the surface.

"It looks like a city ten years after nuclear war," Declan said. "No wonder they want to leave."

Their evil decays the structures.

I looked down at Wally, my brows raised. "Really?"

Like an enhanced version of the grime that coats the buildings in your neighborhood.

I translated for Declan.

"Smart cat you have there."

Hellcat.

"He said he's a hellcat. Likes accuracy, I guess."

"Hellcat." Declan smiled and nodded at Wally. Since I was currently seeing his demon form, it looked weird.

"Do we still look like demons?" I asked Wally.

Ugly as a dog's backside.

"Perfect."

The train ground to a stop, and we rose and followed the crowd of demons out onto the platform. I shifted left and right, trying to avoid brushing my shoulders against theirs.

We stepped into a station that was much smaller than the one we'd already been to—just one ticket booth and one platform.

The demons streamed quickly out of the station, and we followed, stepping out onto a grimy street. Buildings towered high above, and they would have cut out the sun if there had been one. Instead, there was nothing but the black clouds that swirled in the sky. The air was heavy with the feeling of misery and boredom, along with something that felt distinctly like sadism. I couldn't describe what exactly it was that made the air feel like that, but it was almost as if the demons' desire to hurt others was leeching off them and filling the air.

Declan shuddered next to me, a gesture I'd never seen him make before. "Let's be quick."

"Agreed. We'll find a bar, ask for Devyver, then go from there."

It was a simple plan, but the best we could come up with, given that there were no guide books to Dark World.

We hurried across the street, passing a shop that sold nothing but acid. Only in Dark World would the market for acid be so strong that there was a whole shop dedicated to it.

Quickly, we strode down the street. Wally disappeared, but I could feel his presence. I didn't blame him for making himself invisible.

"That looks promising." Declan pointed to a neon sign that was half unlit. It was shaped like a glass of green liquid.

"Yeah, probably a bar."

He entered first. When I stepped through the door and into the tiny bar, my gaze moved quickly over the interior. About half full. Ten people, max, all crowded around little tables and playing a game with black and red cards. The bartender was a bored-looking female demon with short, blunt horns and sharp fangs. At least, I thought she was female. Not that it mattered.

We strode up to the bar, and I reached for one of the coins in my pocket. It was always good form to buy before asking for information. I pointed to a bottle of green liquid that was displayed prominently and held up two fingers.

She nodded and poured into dirty glasses, then pushed them across the bar. "Four durkas."

I handed her the coins and pushed a glass toward Declan. Neither of us drank. No way in hell I'd risk it.

I leaned over the bar. "We're looking for the Devyver."

She gave me a look like I was stupid. "The Devyver?"

"Yeah. Know where he is?" I pushed a coin across the bar.

She snatched it up. "How come you don't know where the Devyver lives?"

"Because we don't?" Shit. Maybe that was weird.

Her brow creased, and a suspicious light entered her eyes.

"We just arrived from the train," Declan said.

"Still, everyone knows where the Devyver lives. Most important guy in Dark World lives in the tallest tower, obviously. Everyone knows that. What's wrong with you?" She inspected us, her eyes flicking suspiciously over our forms.

"Just new here."

"No one is new in Dark World."

From behind, I could hear chairs scraping on the wooden floor.

Shit.

"You feel weird," the bartender said. "Look weird too." She reached below the bar and withdrew a bat covered in spikes.

Well, shit.

7

S hit, these demons were crazy.

"Let's get the hell out of here," I muttered.

We turned, but it was too late. Every demon in the place had crowded in behind us, all ten of them glaring. One was tossing a fireball in his hand, a lazy gesture that made it look like he was about to play a game of summer baseball.

He was, sort of. Except our heads were the targets.

"They look funny," muttered one demon with giant eyes and tiny hands.

"Magic smells weird," said one who had two heads.

I glanced at Declan. "Time to go?"

"Time to go."

I drew my mace from the ether, and he drew a sword. The comforting weight of the chain in my hand made me smile, and I began to swing. The demon closest to me backed up. The one with the fireball snarled and hurled his flame right at my head. I ducked, feeling the heat blaze past me. The sound of shattering glass was followed by the bartender's shriek.

"Careful, guys, or she won't let you back in." I slammed my

mace at the closest demon, crushing his skull. "Not that it'll be a problem for you, since you'll be dead."

Declan lunged for the two nearest him, swinging his blade in a broad arc. He put such force behind it that it sliced both of them in half. Their bodies tumbled, hitting the floor with a series of thuds.

Damn, that angel was strong.

A demon to my left swiped his long claws toward me. They glinted in the dim light, and I jumped back, narrowly avoiding an inconvenient evisceration. I swung my mace toward him, and it slammed into his side. He went down with a howl.

At the back of the bar, Wally had leapt into the air, heading straight for a demon's face. He shot a blast of flame from his mouth that engulfed the demon's head. The creature didn't even scream—just dropped to the ground in silence. Dead.

Shit, my hellcat was scary.

Declan moved like a dancer through the crowd of demons, all deadly grace surrounded by arcs of blood. Impressive, really.

A sound from behind caught my ear, and I turned, swinging my mace. The bartender stood on the counter, her spiked bat raised. My mace smashed into it, shattering the wood and steel.

With an enraged shriek, the bartender jumped on top of me, her hands going straight for my throat. She was fast and strong, slamming me to the ground and squeezing tightly. Pain flared, and I choked.

I dropped the mace chain and called a dagger from the ether, then slammed it into her chest. She hissed and fell backward, and I scrambled away.

Between Wally and Declan, all the patrons were on the ground.

I climbed to my feet. "Okay, time to go!"

We needed to get the hell out of here before law enforcement showed up. If there even was such a thing.

The three of us hurried toward the door, then slowed as we walked through. We turned right and headed up the street, moving as fast as we could without looking suspicious.

"Well, our disguises obviously suck," I said.

"They only stand up from a distance."

"No more questioning, then." I looked up at the sky. "Let's just look for the tallest building, and apparently the most famous demon in the whole place."

The buildings were so close together that it was hard to get a good view of all of them, but eventually we spotted one that was much higher than the rest.

"We can cut through here." I headed toward a darkened street that was more of an alley. It led straight to the tall building we sought.

Declan joined Wally and me, and we strode through, our footsteps silent on the broken asphalt. On either side of us, the buildings rose tall and ominous. These were the first ones we'd seen with intact walls. There were no windows, though.

"Feels like shit in here," Declan said.

I nodded, shivering. The air had a slimy feeling to it, which should be impossible but wasn't.

Meet you on the other side. Don't like it here. Wally disappeared.

"Smart cat," Declan said.

"Hellcat."

"Right, hellcat. I forgot." He grinned, but there wasn't much mirth in it. He probably meant there to be, but the air in this alley was really starting to feel awful.

It made my mind hurt. Made my soul hurt. As if it were sucking all the joy out of the world. My vision started to waver, and I blinked.

"You feel that?" My words came out slurred.

"Yeah." His didn't sound much better.

I staggered onward, my limbs suddenly feeling heavy.

The brick walls on either side wavered, as if images were starting to form on them. Dark rooms, huddled people.

No. One dark room, over and over again. And two huddled girls. Skinny girls—one with blonde hair and one with dark. They were crying.

I gasped, shaking my head to drive away the vision.

But it wouldn't disappear.

Over and over again, I saw myself and Mari during one of our worst nights in Grimrealm. We'd just been forced to try to make more magic—something violent, I recalled—and we'd failed. Aunt had thrown us in the cellar, a dark hole that had always scared us.

Something tightened in my chest, and I gasped, trying to get air into my lungs. Nothing happened. My chest ached.

I staggered, nearly going to my knees.

Declan grabbed me with strong hands, pulling me upright. I leaned on him, squeezing my eyes shut as we stumbled through the ally. But the visions wouldn't fade from my mind, and the air continued to push in on me, suffocating.

I struggled to breathe, trying to get control of myself. I focused on visions of Mari. My friends. Cheetos. Martinis. Anything good in the world.

Finally, I opened my eyes. If I were going to see the visions no matter what, I might as well have them open.

But the vision on the walls was changing—wavering. The young girls were replaced by fields of dying angels. Hundreds of them, bloody and beaten, their wings torn and their limbs broken.

Declan knelt amongst them all, entirely whole and healthy, looking devastated.

Beside me, Declan began to slow. I looked up at him.

His horrified gaze was glued to the images on the wall. I could hear the cries of the men and smell the blood. It felt as if we were *there*. Hell, Declan *was* there. He stopped as he stared at the scene, his face ashen and eyes dark.

Shit.

These had to be our worst memories.

With mine slightly faded, I had more strength. I tugged on Declan's arm. "Come on."

He didn't budge. He didn't go to his knees like I almost had, but he didn't move either. He was frozen in horror.

I yanked on him harder. Nothing.

Damn it.

I slapped him on the cheek, hard.

He shook his head, his eyes clearing. He still looked devastated, but his gaze focused on me. He gave a shuddering sigh. "Thanks."

Together, we staggered through nightmare alley, dragging each other along as we tried to avoid looking at the walls.

Finally, we stumbled out onto an empty street. The images faded.

Wally appeared. *What was it?*

"Nightmares."

Wally shivered. *No souls.*

That would be a nightmare for him.

Declan and I took a moment, catching our breaths and trying to clear our heads.

"That was your childhood?" he asked.

"Don't ask me about my nightmares, and I won't ask you about yours."

"Fair enough."

We all had our secrets, it seemed. I pulled on his arm. "Come on. Let's go find this guy before the people in this miserable place figure out what we are."

He gave me a look that suggested this wasn't over, but he followed.

Wally trotted alongside us. *If we want to make a getaway, we need to get out of the city. Onto the broken plain. Then I can take us home.*

I transferred the message to Declan, who nodded.

Finally, we reached the base of the super tall building. I stared up at it, taking in the open sides that revealed hundreds of rooms.

"Demons aren't really into privacy, are they?" I asked.

"Seems not."

The stairs were built onto the outside of the building, with no railings, of course. They looked rickety and weak in places. The demons took their lives into their hands every time they came home.

"Can we fly up?" Declan asked.

Not if you want to live. None of these demons have wings, so you'll stand out.

I translated for Declan.

"Here goes nothing, then," he said, and stepped onto the first stair. It creaked loudly.

"Definitely no health and safety in the demon world," I muttered.

Declan chuckled and continued up. I followed, stepping gingerly onto the first stair.

Wally raced up the stairs, darting around us and moving quickly and lightly.

We climbed for what felt like forever, passing demon after demon in their homes. Though *homes* was probably an exaggeration—lair was more accurate. Dirty and mostly devoid of furniture. Most of the demons were sleeping in strange nests, and all of them reeked with dark magic. The higher we got, the harder the wind blew. My skin chilled, and I tugged my jacket around me.

The city spread out below us, a miserable vista in shades of brown and gray. The whole place stank of dark magic and evil, and I couldn't imagine living here. Every demon I'd seen had looked fairly content, if bored. Many wanted to go out and make their fortunes on earth, acting as mercenaries tasked with horrible deeds.

I was glad it took a lot of effort to get there. The last thing earth needed was more of these monsters. We had enough of our own.

When a stair broke beneath my foot, it took me a fraction of a second to process what was happening. By the time a scream tore from my throat, I was plummeting through the gap in the stairs.

Frantic, I scrambled for the step in front of me, barely managing to grasp it in time. My legs dangled below, hundreds of feet above the hard ground. I gripped the stair hard and began to haul myself, my palms sweating.

Declan grabbed my wrist and pulled. I gasped, my stomach pitching, as he dragged me up onto the steps between us. I clawed my way up with my free arm until I was on firmer, stronger ground.

"This place is a freaking hazard." I pulled my wrist from Declan's grip, though he seemed hesitant to let go.

"You okay?" Concern shadowed his eyes.

"Besides my heart trying to break my ribs? Yes."

He smiled, pressing his hand to my outer shoulder, the one that was on the side of the open drop to the street below. "My weight must have weakened that step."

I nodded, head still reeling as I tried to catch my breath. There was no safe position in our caravan of two. No matter what, one of us might go through the steps.

Oh, how I wished Wally hadn't warned us against flying.

"I'm fast enough to catch you if you do fall," Declan said.

"Flying?"

He nodded.

It'd be worth it in a pinch, if our lives were at stake.

My heartbeat finally slowed to a bearable level, and I climbed to my feet, keeping my back pressed to the bit of stone wall that still stood on this floor. We'd survive this—as long as Declan had his wings—but it wouldn't be fun. I'd never had a fear of heights, but I wouldn't be surprised if I developed one.

"Let's keep moving."

He nodded and turned, continuing upward. I kept close track of his feet on the steps, listening for any creaking noises that might indicate structural instability.

I was so focused on his feet that I barely noticed the demon coming at us from inside the building. He had a bat in his hands —a spiked bat like the bartender had held, not a baseball bat— and he was headed right for Declan, coming at him from slightly behind.

The angel couldn't see him from this angle.

"Declan! Attack!" I shouted, drawing my sword from the ether. "From your left."

Declan moved impossibly fast, turning to face the demon who was swinging for him. The monster had pale yellow skin with orange eyes and long fangs. He was well muscled and clearly practiced with his weapon.

Declan ducked, narrowly avoiding the spiked bat, and swung his fist for the demon's ugly face. His hand collided with the demon's cheek, and the beast whirled backward and slammed into the ground.

Declan leapt for him and dragged him up by the tattered leather vest he wore. "What the hell is your problem?"

"No one goes up these stairs except the Devyver." He looked upward.

"So, everything past here is his turf?" Declan asked.

The demon nodded, trying to jerk out of Declan's hold while

swinging a clawed hand for his head. Declan slammed his fist into the demon's temple, so hard that the beast slumped, unconscious.

There were still about four stories left before we reached the top, so the Devyver must own all of them.

Declan stood, dusting off his hands and stepping back. He turned to me. "Thanks. He'd have gotten me if not for you."

I nodded, my stomach dropping at the thought of how bad that could have been. If the demon had hit Declan in the head and knocked him out, Declan would have fallen off the stairs and been unable to use his wings.

With a start, I realized that my fists were tightly clenched. I'd been really worried about him. Like, the level of worry that I felt for Mari or my friends.

Oh fates. I was starting to develop feelings for Declan.

I unclenched my fists, stashed my sword in the ether, and drew in a steady breath. "Let's go. I bet he's on the very top."

We continued climbing, trekking quietly up the stairs. The first floor of the Devyver's space was completely empty. The second was full of horrible machines, all hulking metal and twisted wire.

"What the hell are they?" Declan asked.

"No idea." I inspected them without going in. "Some look like steam machinery." I pointed to one that looked like it had the signature boiler and pipes. "But no idea what they are."

This floor felt devoid of life, though, so we continued on.

The next floor was full of body parts. I gagged, stopping dead in my tracks, my eyes glued to the horror within.

Demon parts of all different shapes and sizes—legs, hands, heads, torsos. Magic swirled around each of them, a pale sickly green.

"The magic probably keeps them from decaying," Declan murmured.

"This guy is a monster." I kept going, my soul chilling as we approached the next level.

This one wasn't dissimilar from the last, and the sheer quantity of body parts was enough to really turn my stomach. By the time we reached the top floor, my skin was crawling.

The top level had more signs of life. Though there were body parts scattered all over the place, there were also tables covered in potion-making ingredients, furniture, and a radio playing some kind of horrible scratchy music.

I arched a brow. "Well, we've definitely found the place."

"No kidding."

I stepped into the apartment, the dry wind blowing my hair back from my face.

Declan stuck close to my side, and we entered slowly.

"Hello?" I called. "Devyver?"

There was silence for a moment, then a shuffling sound. An old man appeared from the back of the apartment, his face lined and thin. I liked older people, and usually the idea of threatening one would make me ill.

Not this guy.

His eyes burned with a fanatical, evil light that made my skin crawl.

No wonder he was the most famous person here.

And that's what he was—a *person,* not a demon.

"What the hell?" Declan muttered. "You're human."

The Devyver gave a smile that was devoid of warmth. It chilled me even more than his blank stare. "Almost."

Almost?

I frowned, peering hard at him. There was a blankness to his black eyes—like they were made of onyx instead of belonging to a living person. There was an emptiness to him that I'd never seen before.

"You don't have a soul," I said. "That's it, isn't it?"

"You're right," Declan murmured. "I see it now."

"Right on the first try." The Devyver's creepy smile spread. "Sold it to buy all this." He spread his arms proudly, indicating the horrible workshop.

"But why? Why the hell would anyone live in the Dark World willingly?"

"It's the only place I can practice my craft." An annoyed light entered his dead eyes. "They frowned upon it back on earth."

"Wait, what? You did this on earth?"

"With humans, but demons are so much more fun."

My stomach lurched. Oh shit, this guy was the real deal.

And the demon we were facing had been made by him.

I'd never been so scared of a demon in my life.

Devyver frowned at us. "You're asking too many questions. Demons never ask this many questions."

He'd bought our disguises initially, but he was clever.

He tilted his head. "Your demon image is flickering over your real form."

Crap. Because he was human, he could see through our illusions a bit. Just like Declan and I could see flashes of each other beneath the disguises. It only worked perfectly on other demons.

Devyver hissed and drew something from his pocket. He hurled it at me, but his aim was terrible.

It crashed into the ground a few feet in front of me.

Moron.

A black cloud rose up from it, wafting toward me. It carried hints of despair and misery, along with something that tugged at my mind.

Ah, shit.

He didn't have bad aim at all.

Suddenly, I was back in the cellar with Mari, both of us too young to really understand why Aunt treated us so horribly.

Tears poured down my cheeks, and hunger gnawed at my belly. But the worst was the despair that pulled at my heart. At my soul.

Whatever was in the bomb that the Devyver had thrown, it was triggering my worst memories. Nightmares of my past. I held my breath and staggered forward, keeping my eyes closed as I tried to fight my way out of the horrible cloud.

But the visions kept coming, appearing in my mind's eye as clearly as if I were watching them on TV.

A strong hand gripped mine, and I gasped.

Declan.

Hope surged through me, warm and bright. It began to drive away the awful memories. From the strength of his grip, he was in the midst of remembering something horrible as well.

The scene that I'd seen in nightmare alley?

I steadied myself, trying to escape the memories that threatened to drown me.

I was almost there. Almost free. I could feel it.

Then pain exploded against my skull, and blackness took me.

8

M y head ached like I'd run headfirst into a brick wall, and my mouth was dry as dust. Groggily, I shifted on the hard floor.

Was I hungover?

No, unlikely. I loved a good martini but my hard, partying days were behind me.

And why did my shoulders and wrists ache?

I pried open my eyes, blearily seeing a dusty wooden floor stretched out in front of me.

Crap. I was lying on my side on the floor, my arms bound behind my back. That realization alone spiked my heart rate. I yanked on the restraints, but they were too strong. Some kind of metal, definitely. Probably steel.

I blinked, trying to clear my vision, and spotted an array of people.

No, not people. Body parts. Demon body parts.

Memories crashed into me, and I stiffened, fear icing my skin.

Holy fates, we were in the Devyver's laboratory. The terrifying man was nowhere to be seen, but I doubted he'd gone far. That'd be too lucky.

An icepick of pain stabbed my brain as I twisted my head, searching for Declan. He lay next to me, his temple bloodied and his eyes closed.

Painfully, I scooted across the floor toward him and nudged his head with my own. He groaned.

"Shh." I wished I could put my hand over his mouth.

Slowly, Declan's eyes opened. He looked as groggy as I felt, slowly taking in our surroundings. I could see the moment understanding hit him.

"Shit." The word was quiet as it left his lips.

"Yep." I struggled at my bonds, still unable to break them. I was really freaking strong, but even I couldn't bust my way out of iron shackles.

Cold sweat slicked my skin.

Declan searched the area for a few more seconds, his gaze finally landing on something and narrowing. I turned toward it, my stomach pitching.

The Devyver.

An evil smile stretched across his face as he approached, his black eyes bright with interest. "How did you like my nightmare bomb?"

"Loved it." I gave him a feral grin. "Just as much as I loved nightmare alley."

"That was a bit of my work as well." He smiled proudly. "In truth, I only dabble in that sort of thing. My true passion is creating new creatures." He inspected us coldly. "You'll be one, soon."

Rage and fear burst inside my chest. He was going to chop us up and make us into his weird demon creations?

"Chill," Declan murmured.

Only then did I realize that I was growling. I didn't want to chill, damn it.

But he was right. We needed the Devyver to lower his guard, and me growling like a wolf wasn't going to do that. I sucked down my anger and fear and glared at the Devyver.

"Don't worry," the Devyver said. "Once you've transitioned, you'll like it."

"The hell I will." I gave him my best eat-shit look. It wasn't bad. I knew, since I'd practiced it in the mirror. Along with my ice-queen look and my conciliatory smile for angry customers.

The Devyver chuckled and turned. "I'll be back in a moment. Just need to get the saw."

My stomach pitched. *The saw.*

I looked at Declan. "Is he freaking serious?"

"Monster."

"Monster," I confirmed, jerking at my restraints, making my wrists and shoulders ache.

As soon as the Devyver disappeared into the back of the workshop, Declan sat up.

"You got a plan?" I asked.

"Cross your fingers." His magic swelled on the air, just faintly, bringing with it the scent of a rainstorm and the taste of aged rum. Too faintly for the Devyver to sense it, I prayed.

I peeked behind Declan's back to spot his hands gleaming with heavenly fire. The metal at his wrists melted and dripped to the floor.

"Nice," I whispered.

"He didn't realize what I am."

"Thank fates for that." I scooted around toward him. "Now do me."

"No, I need to find a key."

"No time. Do me."

"The molten metal will burn your wrists."

"I don't care. I have a healing potion. Or you can heal me. But there's *no time.*"

"No." Declan's brow was set in firm lines.

I gave him my hardest look and used my hardest voice. "Do it."

His jaw clenched.

"I'm not going to risk getting turned into some demon Frankenstein because you're scared of hurting a girl. Now do it."

"Not a girl. *You.* I don't want to hurt *you.*"

I just glowered. But maybe—just maybe—a tiny part of my heart melted. Just a little.

"Fine." His jaw tightened even further. "Extend your arms back as far as you can to make them parallel with the floor."

So the molten metal didn't get on my hands, I realized. My stomach lurched. For all my bravado, this was going to *suck.* The molten metal hadn't hurt Declan because he was an angel used to the heat of heavenly fire.

I was just me.

I did as he asked, stretching my arms out. It pulled horribly at my shoulder joints, but I managed to contort myself into a position that would hopefully cause the least amount of damage to my hands and wrists.

"I'll go quickly." Declan's words had barely left his lips before the pain shot through my wrists.

It was so bad I nearly vomited. Then it was gone. My nerve endings were probably destroyed. My head spun, and I tasted blood.

I'd bitten my tongue.

"Done." Declan's soft touch landed on my upper forearms, and relief surged through me. His healing power flooded me with warmth and light as my arms repaired from within.

I drew in steady breaths, trying to ignore the memory of the agony. As his magic flowed into me, mending my flesh, a connection formed between us. Just like it had the last time—magic or emotion or desire or *something*. And I liked it.

A lot.

Time seemed to slow.

Unconsciously, I leaned back toward him, images of kissing him flowing through my mind. Our last kiss—our *only* kiss—had been amazing, sweeping me off my feet and making my heart race.

Oh fates, I wanted to do that again.

Every inch of me prickled with awareness—of him. He was close. The heat of his body nearly burned my back. Or maybe it was my imagination.

Either way, I wanted to kiss him. That desire *wasn't* imaginary.

Finally, Declan removed his hands. "All better."

His voice was rough, as if he'd felt it, too.

I pulled my arms around to look at them, relieved to see my wrists looking normal. Then looked up at him.

There was heat in his eyes that probably reflected my own. I swallowed hard, my eyes glued to his lips, and tried to think of anything but kissing him. There was something about the connection formed by his healing light that turned me on, but this was easily the worst place in the universe to become distracted by a kiss.

"Glad I didn't have to see it happen," I finally said, my gaze moving over the rest of the room.

"You should be."

I looked back to see that a stark expression had replaced the one of desire on Declan's face. He was remembering watching my flesh melt, and he hadn't liked it, clearly.

"Thanks."

He nodded. "Let's lie back down. Get him by surprise."

I nodded and did as he suggested, careful to avoid the still hot metal that was eating through the wooden floor. We resumed our slumped positions and waited.

It wasn't long before the Devyver returned, a pep in his step that belied his age. Honestly, given the magic he was capable of, he could be *any* age.

"Ready?" he asked, coming closer, a jagged saw gripped in his hand.

There was no way he planned to start cutting us up without binding our legs. I studied the rest of him, spotting a little potion bomb clutched in his hand. There was a similar-sized bulge in his jacket pocket.

Probably a sedative of some kind.

"Left hand," I whispered.

Declan nudged his shoulder against mine to confirm that he'd heard.

The Devyver was only about five feet away when I took my chance, lunging for him. He raised the hand that held the glass potion bomb, but I was quicker, smacking his fist so the little glass ball crashed on the floor.

I kicked the saw out of his hand and got him in a headlock with his hands behind his back.

He shrieked, "Guards!"

Shit.

"I got 'em." Declan's voice cut through the sound of approaching footsteps.

A dozen horrifying creatures approached, each made of different parts of demons. They were all colors and shapes, carrying all manner of weapons.

Declan drew a sword from the ether and darted toward them.

I was done fooling around.

I dragged the Devyver toward the empty space where a wall should've been, then slung his body over, grabbing his arm at the last minute. He dangled hundreds of feet in the air, his face shocked and his black eyes wide.

"We need to know how to control an Oraxia demon," I said. "To command its loyalties."

The man hissed at me.

"I will drop you in a heartbeat. I *want* to."

"Then you'll never get what you came for!"

I shrugged, making my voice cold. "I'm an excellent blood sorceress and quite clever, if I do say so myself. I bet I can figure it out if I'm given enough time in your workshop."

"You won't!"

I shot a glance at the fight that raged behind me. Declan stood between me and the small army of demons, attacking them as they approached, giving me time to question the Devyver.

I looked back at the Devyver. "If you want to live, you need to give me what I want."

"It's nearly impossible."

I shook him, making his whole body wobble in the wind and his face pale even more. "If I don't get what I want..."

I dipped him low, extending my arm so he dropped a bit.

"I'll do it! I'll do it!" he shrieked. "There's a way, and I can tell you!"

"Good. We just have to wait until my buddy takes out your crazy monsters."

Horror flashed in his eyes. "No! My children!"

"Dude, don't even try to play on my emotions." I bared my teeth at him in a facsimile of a smile. "I don't have any."

He whimpered, and I gave him a real smile.

I enjoyed this, actually.

Quickly, I checked on Declan. There were half a dozen demons left, but he had it under control.

I turned back to the Devyver. "Did you sic your Oraxia demon on Magic's Bend?"

"No!"

Damn it.

I believed him.

I shook him anyway, just to be sure. One last chance to make sure he was scared enough to tell the truth. "I'll drop you."

"I haven't seen an Oraxia demon in years. The last one left ten years ago."

"So someone found him and hired him?"

"It's likely. They're some of the best mercenaries out there." He smiled proudly, and my stomach turned.

But I did believe him. He wasn't our mastermind. He was too obsessed with his work here, anyway.

I looked back at Declan. There were only a couple demons left, and he cut through them quickly.

I yanked the Devyver back up. "You need better guards."

"No one attacks me here." He tried to shake off my grip on his wrist, but I didn't let go. Touching him made me cringe, but I couldn't risk it.

"You have to let me go so I can make you the potion to control the Oraxia demon. They're special. Nothing like these prototypes." He gestured to the bodies dismissively. "Without the potion, you don't stand a chance."

I didn't want to let him go entirely, just in case he tried to pull a fast one. My gaze caught on wall covered in metal bits and bobs. There was a small loop of metal attached to a chain.

My stomach lurched in recognition.

A neck manacle.

Ew.

But useful.

I pointed to it and looked at Declan. "Can you get me that, please?"

He brought it over and snapped it around the Devyver's neck. The monster-maker looked at me, insulted.

"This is the least of what I'll do to you." I grabbed the end of the chain and shook it. "Now that I've got ahold of you, tell me what we're going to need."

Declan stepped up to him, looming over him and flaring his wings wide.

"Fallen angel!" The Devyver gasped, fear widening his eyes.

"Indeed. And if I want, I can find that soul you sold."

The Devyver swallowed hard.

"So, you'll tell us the truth. Because if we're not successful, I'm going to get that soul. Then I'm going to feed it to her hellcat."

Wally appeared, as if he'd heard his name called. He hissed, arching his back, and his flame-red eyes flared bright.

The Devyver's gaze fell on Wally, and he turned so pale that he was nearly transparent.

He nodded and stuttered, "I—I can do that."

"Good." Declan gave him a cold smile. "Now tell us what we need to know to control the Oraxia demon. And what the bastard looks like."

Wally strolled toward the Devyver, who couldn't get the words out fast enough. "First, you need a potion starter. I can make that." He nodded frantically, a promising look on his face. "Then, you need to get a rare ingredient from Eleuthera, in the Bermuda Triangle."

Shit. "What?"

He turned his gaze to me. "I told you that it would not be easy. If it were easy to get that ingredient, I would have it."

"What is it?" I asked.

"A sea sapphire. They are located at the bottom of a cave on the island, which is hidden from the eyes of humans."

"Where is the cave?" Declan asked.

"The north end of the island. It's called Pirate's Cave, and it's been abandoned for hundreds of years. But that's not all you need. You must also get a piece of the Oraxia demon that you are trying to control."

"A piece?" I frowned.

"Yes, you know. Like a hair or nail or finger or eye."

Of course it involved a body part. I shouldn't have expected anything different from a guy like the Devyver.

"You'll put those two ingredients into the potion starter that I give you and shake it up. Then splash the potion onto the demon, and you can command him."

"Will our commands override previous commands?" Declan asked.

"They will. Though he will be fighting between two loyalties, so it won't be easy to control him."

"Fine." But we could work with this. I shook the chain. "Get to work on the potion starter."

He frowned and tugged on the chain. "Give me more slack."

I gave him a bit more, but not much, then followed him around the workshop as he gathered ingredients. Most of them were glass jars filled with colorful mist that swirled and sparkled.

Wally disappeared, as if he knew his job was done.

The Devyver took his stash to a fire pit in the middle of the apartment. It flickered brightly, orange and yellow. There was a hole in the ceiling to release the smoke.

No wonder he had the top floor of the building. Given the open walls and lack of vegetation, I had a feeling that it never rained here.

"I'm watching you." I gave my voice an ominous tone, and shook the chain. "Don't forget about the hellcat."

"All right. *All right.*" He sounded peeved as he got to work, opening the vials of colorful mists right over the top of the fire.

I stared hard at him, analyzing his expression and his movements for any sign of deception. I didn't want him pulling a fast one and creating something to hurt us.

They didn't dissipate into the air as I'd expected. Instead, they swirled over the orange fire, forming colorful balls of mist.

"What kind of magic is this?" Declan demanded.

"The kind you sell your soul for."

Ugh. This whole business was shady.

Finally, the mist seemed to be slowing. The Devyver pulled a tiny stone jar out of his pocket. He held it beneath the swirling mist, and after a moment, the mist turned to liquid and fell into the jar. He corked it and handed it to me with a strange smile. "That will work."

I took it, studying the look on his face. There was something off about it. "It had better, or I'm coming back for you." I hiked a thumb at Declan. "Him too. With your soul and my hellcat."

The Devyver shivered, fear clear in his eyes. He shifted, obviously uncomfortable.

What the hell was up with him?

"What does the demon look like?" Declan asked.

"All Oraxia demons are complete. Not made of parts, like those." He pointed to the guards that Declan had felled. "Tall and strong, with orange skin, black eyes, and four horns."

Four horns were rare on a demon.

"Do they have any weaknesses?" I asked.

A wide smile stretched across his face. "No."

"No?" Declan sounded incredulous.

"No, they don't." The smile widened even farther.

I yanked on his chain. "Tell us the truth."

He smiled. "I am. The Oraxia demon was one of my greatest accomplishments. I was only able to make three as I had a limited supply of Leviathan Weed, but those three demons are surrounded by a forcefield that no magic can penetrate."

"Bullshit," Declan said.

I studied the Devyver—his cocky smile, the relaxed set of his shoulders, the glow shining from his face. This was the reason for his weird expression a moment ago. "No, he means it. He really means it."

"I've never heard of Leviathan Weed," Declan said.

"It's a myth." I searched my mind for all that I recalled of it. "Or at least, I thought it was a myth. Turns out this little weasel found some of it."

"Indeed, I did. Took all there was, too. And the weed imbued the Oraxia demon with a defensive shell that no magic can penetrate."

"So, the potion that you made for us," Declan said. "It will be impossible for us to get a piece of his body in order to complete the potion and the spell."

The Devyver laughed.

Anger bubbled in my chest. This jerk. He was destroying lives with his work.

"A nullifier could get through the Oraxia demon's shell," Declan said.

The Devyver's eyes widened, then narrowed. "Yes, one could." He shrugged. "*If* you can find one."

Which we probably couldn't. Nullifiers were a type of Magica who could undo magic. They were *extremely* rare. About five years ago, my friend Cass found one.

He'd died. I thought she'd taken his power, but it was such a miserable magic to possess that she'd gotten rid of it immediately.

"We'll find one," Declan said.

The Devyver laughed.

I yanked hard on his chain again.

He held up his hands in a placating gesture. "Fine, fine."

I looked at Declan. "Let's get the hell out of here."

He nodded, expression grim. "About time."

I turned to the Devyver and punched him so hard he flew backward, then lay still. Declan knelt over him.

"Dead?" I asked. That'd been one powerful punch.

"Looks that way."

"Good." Most of my friends didn't like killing. I didn't mind it —at least, not with the right sorts.

And the Devyver was definitely the right sort. Made of evil and just creating more of it. He actively worked to make the world a more horrible place.

We left the Devyver where he lay and descended the stairs again, taking them two at a time on our way down.

"Will Wally meet us when we're out of town?" Declan asked.

"I think so." The hellcat had said we had to be outside of the town before his magic could transport us out of there, but how far outside?

We were halfway down the stairs when a gong rang, loud and clear. It came from the top floor, and my skin chilled.

"Wasn't he dead?" Declan asked.

"I thought so. Someone may have found him."

"Faster." Declan picked up the pace, but the alert was out.

A demon roused from its nest in the open-air apartment next to us and looked at us, hissing. It lunged upright, headed for us.

Damn it. That gong had definitely been an alarm.

I called my mace and chain from the ether and swung it toward the approaching demon. He ducked, avoiding the first strike, but the mace came back around and slammed him in the head.

I sprinted after Declan, who'd had to stop on the stairs below me to fight off two demons who'd come out of their own apartments. Another one came for me from the floor above. He was tall and skinny, with long claws and fangs. He swiped for me, and I ducked, nearly losing my footing on the narrow stairs.

My stomach lurched as I spotted the ground, far below. I sucked in a deep breath and looked back up at the demon, shoving away my fear.

I swung my mace and hit him in the middle, bowling him over. Declan sliced down the two demons who'd come for him—each of them well over six feet tall and heavily muscled—but more were charging up the stairs toward us.

Apparently the whole place went on the alert when the alarm rang.

Below, the streets heaved with activity. Demons were pouring out of the other buildings and looking up toward us.

Holy fates, the whole *city* was after us.

"Screw this." Declan's black wings flared from his back. "They've already figured out we're not like them, so let's get out of here."

I sprinted down toward him, taking the last few stairs in a rush. I stashed my mace in the ether and leapt into his arms. He gripped me tightly and took off, just as a fire demon hurled a blast of flame at us. It nearly hit Declan in the leg, but he kicked it away with his boot.

"Go straight up!" I shouted, drawing a shield from the ether. It'd make it easier for me to block oncoming magic with my shield, otherwise the firebombs and icicles could hit Declan in the back.

Declan shot for the sky, his powerful wings carrying us high.

I leaned over in his arms, grateful for his strong grip on me, and held the shield so it deflected the worst of the magic hurled at us. It was awkward as hell and we both got hit in the legs a few times, but we made it out of range without serious injury.

"Get ready to call your hellcat." Declan grinned and flew fast, heading for the edge of town. The whole city was surrounded by a wasteland of barren ground cut through with crevasses. The train tracks heading back to the station were empty. The train was long gone.

Please show up, Wally.

Finally, we reached the edge of the city. Down below, demons chased us, sprinting as a horde. Thank fates we were up here in the sky.

As soon as I thought it, something huge and gray hurtled toward us, shooting down from above us. It was the size of my car, with a massive beak and sharp claws. Tattered gray fabric fluttered from its wings.

"A shroud bird!" I shouted, my skin chilling. I'd only ever heard of them, but thought they were myths.

Apparently not, and they were deadly.

Two more appeared behind it, headed straight for us. The closest bird shrieked, a blast of freezing air shooting from its beak. The air wasn't just cold, according to myth. It also carried the winds of death.

"We do *not* want that bird to breathe on us! Go lower!"

Declan didn't need to be told twice. He dived for the ground. I looked up, heart thundering in my ears. The bird raced down toward us, tattered gray wings flapping hard on the air.

The air was their domain. If we could get to the ground, we might have a chance.

I looked down, trying to gauge our distance from safety, and spotted an army right below us.

Shit. We were trapped.

9

"Are you sure about this?" Declan demanded.

"No!" I looked back up at the bird, who was closer. Only fifty feet away, if that. He was so damned big and his breath sparkled with icy cold.

Dread stole my breath.

Down below, the demons were following us, running across the barren ground outside the city.

Yeah, better to take our chances down there. At least we were outside of the city limits. As long as Wally showed up right away, we'd be good.

"Go to the ground!" I shouted.

"All right." He sounded skeptical, but he trusted me, flying fast for the ground.

He flew at an angle, gaining a bit of a lead on the crowd of demons. I kept my gaze glued to the three shroud birds above, riveted to the sight of their icy breath.

"Almost there," Declan said.

The birds veered off, heading back up to the sky.

"It worked!"

Declan hit the ground with a thud, and I leapt out of his arms. "Wally!"

"Wally!" I didn't know how to call the hellcat to me, but I hoped this worked.

A firebomb plowed into the dirt next to me, and I turned to catch sight of the demons sprinting after us. They were only about one hundred feet away.

"Run!" Declan sprinted away from them.

I followed, my legs wobbly from the hits I'd taken when we'd flown away from the Devyver's building. "Wally!"

We sprinted fast, darting left and right as we tried to outrun the icicles and firebombs. My lungs felt like they would burst, but I gave it my all, racing away from the demons.

A fireball glanced off my thigh, and pain bloomed.

I screamed, desperate. "Wally!"

Finally, the black hellcat showed up, running alongside.

Where are we going?

"Home!"

Then stop running!

I stopped, shouting, "Declan, stop!"

He halted, spinning back to run toward me, his expression saying I was crazy. Then he spotted Wally. "Thank fates."

I drew a shield from the ether, and Declan did the same. We turned to face the oncoming demons, ducking behind our shields.

Blasts of magic slammed into the metal protection, shaking my arms and nearly bowling me over.

Declan's magic swelled, and lightning began to strike from the sky, hitting the demons one after the other. They fell, but others took their places, stomping on the bodies of the fallen as they charged us.

Wally weaved around our legs, his smoky form expanding and enclosing us as the cloud grew bigger. I watched the demons with wide eyes, holding my shield up to deflect the blows that landed with more accuracy as they got closer. Declan's lightning was working, but there were just too many of them.

"Come on, Wally!" My heart thundered as we waited for the hellcat's magic to take effect. It was probably only a few seconds at most, but holy fates, my heart felt like it would jump out of my throat.

It's hard here. Dark World is the farthest place from earth.

The demons were close enough that I could make out their features. Close enough that they'd be on us in seconds.

Shit.

I called upon my magic, slicing my thumb with my finger. Blood welled, and I imagined controlling the earth, praying that Declan wouldn't notice what I was doing. I'd try to make it look natural.

In front of us, the ground began to crack. It took everything I had to command the earth to move. This was big magic—bigger magic than I usually used my dragon blood for. I poured my power into it, feeling the drain on my strength.

The crack widened, and the demons slowed.

Yes.

Declan glanced at me. "Is that you?"

"No, we must have gotten lucky. There are so many cracks in this land, and one is forming here."

Okay, that was total bullshit. Yes, there were a lot of cracks in the land. But what were the odds one would appear right in front of us?

Shit. Those were the odds. Pure shit.

A skeptical frown creased Declan's face, but it faded when the first demon leapt over the crack. Then another. And another.

Almost there.

The ether began to tug at me, just slightly. "Come on, Wally, you can do it."

Finally, when the demons were only yards away, Wally's magic kicked in.

Thank fates. I was totally drained.

The ether grabbed me and pulled me through space, spinning me wildly as we returned home.

The ether spat me out in the parking lot of our favorite beach, just north of town. It was daylight here, with the sun hiding behind some clouds. Declan and Wally appeared next to me.

Panting, I crouched and looked in Wally's flame-red eyes. "Thanks, pal. You're the best."

He purred and rubbed against my hand, then walked away. *Off to find some dinner.*

I didn't know where he went to find the souls he ate, and I definitely didn't want to. I stood and turned to Declan. "*That* was close."

"No kidding."

I patted my pocket to make sure that the vial of potion was still there, and smiled. I looked at Declan. "Give me a second, I need to change."

He nodded, and I hurried off toward a collection of trees. Quickly, I took my ghost suit from the ether and changed my clothes, making sure to tuck the vial of potion back into my pocket. Once the familiar material settled onto my shoulders, I relaxed the smallest bit. I was a creature of habit, and I liked my ghost suit. I'd wear something else when the situation was dire, but only if I had to.

Properly dressed, I returned to Declan. I had Bree's clothes tucked into my arm, and I'd have to stash them in my car until I saw her again.

"Do you know a nullifier?" The problem had been spinning around my head this whole time.

He shook his head. "Maybe the Protectorate can find one. I can call some contacts, too."

I nodded. "Good. And we have some serious firepower here. The DragonGods are mega strong. There's a good chance they can get through the magical barrier that protects the Oraxia demon."

He squeezed my arm. "We'll make it work."

We had to.

I pressed my fingertips to the comms charm at my throat. "Mordaca? Where are you? How's the evac going?"

"Hey. We're at the beach."

"The beach?" I turned to inspect the parking lot, then headed toward the water. Declan followed. "We're here, too. But why are you?"

"It's right at the six-hour mark," she said. "All evacuation crews have cleared out of town for thirty minutes until we know which district is frozen."

My heard thudded. "Oh crap, it's already been six hours?"

"Twelve. You were gone a long time."

My stomach pitched. Shit. "What district fell?"

"Business."

"Crap. And now you're waiting to hear about the other?"

"Exactly."

I spotted her striding up the beach in her black fight suit, her eyes weary but her hair and makeup still perfect. She pressed her comms charm to sever the connection and shouted, "How'd it go?"

"We've got a lead and a problem."

A moment later, we met on the sand. Closer to the water, a couple dozen Protectorate members were sitting on logs and eating sandwiches.

"We're about to head back in," Mari said. "As soon as we hear which district has been hit."

"How's it going?" Declan asked. "Are people leaving?"

Mari shrugged. "They're stubborn. We made a citywide announcement that played in everyone's homes, but we're going door to door, and we've discovered many people who didn't leave."

"Can you make them?" Declan asked.

"No. But we can strongly encourage, and it's working in a lot of cases. Once someone is there to scare the crap out of them in person, they'll usually get the message and leave." Her gaze turned sad. "But mostly we're just helping those who couldn't afford to leave or didn't have the ability. Like older people and poor people. Sick people. Those with animals."

I looked at Declan. "There's not any public transportation out of town because there isn't another all-magical city for hundreds of miles."

Understanding dawned. "So a lot of people would be stranded."

"Exactly." Evacuating was a privilege. It was the same in the human world. I'd seen it on the news, with things like hurricanes and other natural disasters.

"What's your plan?" Mari asked. "What did you find out?"

I decided to start with the good news and explained about the Bermuda Triangle and the ingredients that we were looking for. "Can you transport us there?"

She shook her head. "No. It's a blank space. No one can. You *may* be able to transport out, but since it's constantly moving, it's impossible for a transporter to find it. I think you'll need a boat."

Fates, that would be slow.

Her eyes met mine. "You mentioned some bad news, and I have a feeling you led with the good. What's the damage?"

"The Devyver doesn't know who hired the Oraxia demon, so

we still don't know who the mastermind is." It was a shadow that hung over us—*who* the hell had planned this?

"That's not all," Mari said. "I can tell there's more."

I nodded. "The demon was made using Leviathan Weed."

Figuring out who wanted all of Magic's Bend turned to stone was our biggest problem. But the fact that the Oraxia demon was unbeatable? That was our most *immediate* problem.

She frowned, her brow creased as she searched her memory. "The stuff that makes you invincible? That's a myth."

"Apparently not."

"Shit." She paled.

"We need a nullifier," Declan said. "If the DragonGods and our combined firepower can't make a dent in the Oraxia demon's shell, a nullifier is the only one who can undo the magic that makes him invincible."

Mari's eyes widened. Memories swirled in their depths, but she managed to keep her voice calm when she said, "We'll ask the Protectorate if they know one. We have about twelve hours. We'll find one."

"I'll ask my contacts as well," Declan said. "Because if we don't find one, and we can't get through the demon's protective shell, we're screwed."

I shivered. He was right. If we failed to defeat him, he would deploy his last orb, and we'd be turned to stone since we'd be in the same vicinity.

"We'll manage," Mari said. She met my gaze again, and I nodded imperceptibly. We had a lot to talk about, and I didn't want Declan to overhear. I looked at him. "Would you get me a sandwich from over by the fire? I'm famished."

His eyes narrowed, as if he knew I was up to something.

Which I totally was, so points to him.

"Please," I added.

Finally, he nodded, then strode off toward the fire.

I leaned close to Mari, whispering quickly, "If we can't find a nullifier, I'll create the magic. I'll become one."

"Creating just a little bit of nullifying magic probably won't be enough," she said. "One little swipe of your fingernail to your thumb won't be enough blood. Not if he's that powerful. Nullifying is huge magic. You'd need to go big. Maybe make it permanent."

I shivered. With our dragon blood power to create magical skills, more blood equaled stronger magic. If we gave so much blood we nearly died, then the new magical skill would be ours permanently.

With all the downsides, like an increased magical signature that could eventually signal what we were.

"I know," I said. "But I'll do it if I have to."

"No. You can't create new magic—not on a big scale. It could change your magical signature. Make it so much stronger and put you at risk of discovery. People could know what you are."

"It's a risk I have to take."

Her eyes flashed, and it was clear she was searching for ways to convince me this was a bad idea.

Hell, I agreed it was a bad idea. I also thought that it might be the *only* idea.

"Remember what happened to Cass?" she said. "That was *awful*."

I nodded, my stomach pitching. Cass, who was now frozen in stone, had once taken a nullifier's power. She hadn't wanted to, but it had been the only way to save Mari's life. To save the lives of many.

The consequences had been devastating.

A nullifier's power not only nullified all other magic, it nullified your own as well, crushing all the other power that you had in your soul. Cass had once told me that it felt like her soul had been sucked from her body.

Cass had looked like a walking husk.

"I can't let you do this," Mari said. "*I'll* do it."

"*No.* You carried the burden when we were children, protecting me. You made more magic than I did." The memory of it made me shudder.

"I don't care," Mari said.

"Well, *I* do. It's my turn now." I squeezed her hand. "And remember—this is a gradient thing. More blood equals more magic. I'll try to make it so that I'm a weak nullifier with partial power. Perhaps it won't crush the rest of my magic. I'll be just strong enough to defeat the Oraxia demon."

"You don't know if that will work."

"I don't know what else will."

Her eyes turned serious. "You're forgetting the last bit."

I swallowed hard, hoping she wouldn't remember.

"Immortality." Her expression turned grave.

"There's no guarantee that will happen." Immortality wasn't the gift it sounded like. Not to me, at least. I didn't want to live forever without Mari. Without my friends.

Mari's eyes flashed to a spot behind me, and I turned. Declan approached. I looked back at Mari.

She squeezed my hand. "We'll find one. I'll talk to the Protectorate."

"Thanks."

Declan stopped next to me and handed me a sandwich.

I took it. "Thanks."

Mari's phone buzzed in her pocket. She pulled it out and pressed it to her ear, saying a few words. I ate while she talked. I really had been famished.

When she hung up, she looked at us, her face pale. "The Museum District is frozen. An overhead search confirms it."

"Right at the six-hour mark." Damn. That gave us twelve more hours before the last two districts were frozen and the whole town was permanently lost. "Had you gotten to that district yet for evacuation?"

"Only half of it." Her voice was devastated.

I gripped her hand. "We can fix this. Don't worry."

"We have to." She straightened her shoulders. "Now that it's safe to head back in, I'm going to rally the troops. We need to keep working. Just in case..."

Just in case Declan and I failed.

If we couldn't stop the Oraxia demon in time, the only people who would survive would be those who evacuated.

"Just in case." I gave her a hug. "Safe hunting."

"Safe hunting." She returned to the crowd, who'd all stood, as if they'd seen her on the phone and sensed that now was the time.

I turned to Declan. "We need a boat to get through the Bermuda Triangle. Got one?"

"No. Not much of a sailor."

"Me neither, as much as I love the ocean." We had absolutely no time to research and find someone with a boat who was willing to take us to the most dangerous part of the ocean. So we needed someone with a stake in this. "What about that woman who captained the ferry? She's probably from Magic's Bend. She'll want to save her town."

"Her boat is in the Pacific, though."

I shrugged. "We need a willing supernatural captain more than we need a boat. We can always steal one of those in Florida."

He nodded, resigned. Clearly he didn't like the idea of stealing a boat, but we had a town to save. "If we have to steal one, we can always pay them later."

"Exactly. Now, let's go. The marina is super close, and hopefully we'll get lucky."

We hurried back to the car, which we'd left here before we'd gone to Dark World, and I drove to the marina, my foot pressed hard to the gas. The road on the other side—the one going out of Magic's Bend—was packed with a steady stream of evacuees. No one was going my direction.

"It's eerie," I said.

"Town will be even eerier."

I shuddered to think of it. All of those people, turned to stone. Maybe forever.

No. We *would* succeed.

A few minutes later, I pulled into the parking lot at the marina. A lot of the boats were gone. People were getting the hell out of Dodge.

At the very end, the ferryboat rocked gently on the waves, tugging at its ropes. It was the same one as before—about one hundred feet long with two stories of cabins.

I breathed a sigh of relief. "It's still here."

"Hopefully she is, too."

"I think she lives on board." I climbed out of the car, my eyes glued on the boat. A small figure untied the rope at the bow and jumped on.

Shit.

"I think she's taking off." I sprinted toward her, racing down the dock. "Hey! Stop!"

The figure didn't seem to hear me as she strode toward the captain's wheelhouse. Or maybe she didn't care.

I ran faster, lungs burning. "Stop!"

The ferry began to pull away from the dock. I gave it my all, sprinting like I was going for gold. The ferry was a few feet away from the dock when I reached it. I didn't even slow, just leapt onto the boat and grabbed onto the railing to keep from falling into the harbor.

I nearly slipped and crashed into the water, but got a good grip at the last second. I clung to the railing, panting.

Declan joined me, leaping easily onto the boat.

"Hey!" The captain's voice sounded, but she didn't appear. She probably had to stay at the wheel while we were still close to the dock and other boats.

Quickly, I climbed over the railing and hurried to her.

She was leaning out of the little room with the steering wheel, her red curls wild about her face. The goofy captain's hat sat on her head. "What are you doing here?" She squinted. "Hey, didn't I give you a ride to Supernalito?"

"You did. And now we need your help."

She gave me a skeptical look. "With what? And may I remind you, you're a stowaway."

"We'll pay," Declan said. "But we need to get to the island of Eleuthera in the Bermuda Triangle."

She laughed loudly, suddenly looking even younger. I'd peg her at about twenty-two. She was a good captain, despite her age, though. She'd gotten us through a pretty rough patch the last time we'd sailed with her.

Finally her laughter trailed off. "Why the hell would I go there? Do I look like I have a death wish?"

10

I gave the boat captain my most serious look, trying to impress upon her the dire nature of the situation. "The only way to save Magic's Bend is if we go to Eleuthera. And we can only get there if a boat takes us. You're the only captain we know."

I explained the situation with the statues, the demon, the potion, and our time limit.

She frowned, irritation and worry glinting in her eyes. "I didn't want to get involved."

"Dozens of people will die if we don't do something," Declan said. "Hundreds, maybe."

She swallowed hard, shifting on her feet. Clearly, she was waffling.

"You'd be a hero," I said.

"Don't really care about that." She pursed her lips. "But I am your best shot. I'm a damned good captain."

I liked her confidence. "You *are* our only hope. We don't know how to find another captain in time."

She frowned, dropping her head as she leaned over the big wooden steering wheel. "Damn it. Another captain would need to be supernatural. Those are the only kinds who can get through the worst parts of the Bermuda Triangle. You need to know what's coming. How to get out."

"And you can do that. Think of all the people," I begged. "Please."

"Fine." She scowled. "Fates, I hate this." She met my gaze. "But we're going to need to get a boat over in Miami or Fort Lauderdale. You got one?"

"Um…" I looked around for the right words. "We'll get one."

She groaned. "You're going to steal one, aren't you?"

I gave a helpless shrug. "We don't really have time to buy one."

"I can't go to jail. I am *not* cut out for the slammer."

"You look like you could hold your own," I said.

"Well, duh. But I gotta run free. Like a stallion."

If the situation hadn't been so dire, I might have laughed.

"And I got a conscience, you know," she said.

"We'll try to take the boat of an asshole. Sound good?" I asked. "*And* we'll leave them some money."

"I don't like it any more than you do," Declan said. "But we have twelve hours to fix this. We have no time to spare with buying a boat or finding another captain. This is our only chance. *You* are our only chance."

She scowled, as if she didn't like being reminded of it. Then she brightened. "Hang on. I know just the boat."

"Yeah?" I asked.

"Owned by a total asshole. A playboy mage who's a real jerk. Owns three boats, all over the world. Rumored to be a drug lord."

"Drug lord?" Oh, man.

"Yep. We'll steal his boat in Miami. I know where he keeps it."

"Hell yeah." I could totally get behind this.

"Do you have a transport charm?" she asked.

"Yeah."

"Good. Let me get this old girl back into port, then we can go." She rubbed her hands together and looked at me. "Actually, I like a bit of adventure."

I grinned. "I can promise you adventure."

It didn't take long to steer the boat back to its berth, and Declan and I helped tie it off, jumping onto the dock when she pulled into her spot.

The captain strode toward us, and I realized I didn't know her name.

I stuck out my hand. "I'm Aerdeca, by the way."

She shook. "I'm Syra."

"Declan." He leaned forward, hand outstretched.

She and Declan shook, then he pulled a transport charm out of his pocket. He handed it to her. "You do the honors, since you know where we're going."

"Come on," she said. "I have shit aim. Let's get off the dock."

I looked down at the wooden slats upon which I stood. There was about a half inch of space between each piece of wood, and I could see the water beneath.

Yeah, getting onto solid ground was smart. We followed her toward the parking lot.

I leaned toward Declan. "How many more of those do you have?"

"One."

"Same." So we only had two more shots. There was always Wally, but his magic took a little while.

We reached the parking lot, and Syra stopped, turning to look at us. "Ready?"

We both nodded.

"Then let's get this party started." She hurled the stone to the ground. Gray sparkling smoke rose up, and we stepped into it.

The ether sucked me in and spun me around, then spit me out in the middle of a huge marina. Declan and Syra appeared next to me.

The hot Florida sun beat down upon my head, and I shielded my eyes, looking around. It was probably the middle of the afternoon here, and the marina was largely empty. Lots of boats rocking on the turquoise water, but only a few people.

"Is it a weekday?" I'd totally lost track of time.

"Monday." Syra grinned. "As good a time as any to steal a boat. Better than the weekend, actually. Come on."

She started off toward the docks. There had to be a couple hundred boats floating on the brilliant blue water. They were all shapes and sizes, but when I realized that she was heading toward a big powerboat that looked like it could travel at light speed, I grinned. "*That's* the boat."

The smile on her face was so big it was nearly blinding. "Yep. Drug runners need fast boats."

"I don't think we should pay him for this thing," I said. "Two birds with one stone—we get transportation to Eleuthera to save Magic's Bend, and we deal a crippling blow to a drug lord."

"I'm all right with that." Declan looked at Syra. "If it's widely known that this boat belongs to a drug lord, why doesn't the Order of the Magica do something about it?"

"He pays them off." She looked like she wanted to spit. "Weasel."

Anger rose in my chest. "Bastards. They're supposed to protect people."

"They do protect people," Syra said. "Themselves."

"Well, this guy is about to be out of a boat."

The powerful speedboat sat low to the water, with a sharply pointed bow and little windows in the hull. It was one of those that looked mostly flat all the way across the middle and front, but there was a cabin inside. The wheel was at the back, in a nice cockpit with benches and two chairs near the steering wheel. As much as I loved the ocean, I'd never learned much about boats.

I slowed my approach, spotting a shadow passing behind one of the small windows. A person. "There's someone in there."

Syra frowned. "I guess I'm not surprised. Probably one of his goons."

Another shadow caught my eye. "Actually, there's two."

"We'll take care of them," Declan said. "Let's get them by surprise. They're still inside."

We hurried toward the boat, striding along at just short of a run. This was a human and supernatural marina—we didn't need to draw attention.

Syra led the way, leaping onto the back of the boat with ease. It was a spacious seating area with plush benches and two golden wood tables permanently affixed to the deck. The steering wheel was just in front, with two tall chairs bolted to the ground.

"Hey!" A voice sounded from down below, in the cabin.

I rushed toward it, wanting the fight to go down inside the boat where no one could see.

A figure appeared in the door to the cabin. He was tall and skinny, with greasy dark hair and pale blue eyes. Small horns protruded from his head, barely visible. A demon who almost passed as human.

Good. Made it easier that way. I didn't like killing humans, even evil ones.

I neared, getting a hit of his signature. His magic stank of rotten garbage and old socks. He raised a hand that glowed with flame.

"That guy is one of his main henchmen," Syra said. "Donnie the Beater."

Oh, I didn't like that name. It was easy to guess what role he played in the drug business. I drew a dagger from the ether just as Donnie hurled his fireball at me. I ducked, feeling the heat singe the top of my hair. It whizzed overhead, and I heard a sizzling sound as it crashed into the water behind me.

Hopefully no one saw that.

I chucked my dagger, aiming straight for the neck. It plunged into the pale white column, spurting blood.

As soon as Donnie fell, Declan leapt over his body and collided with the man who'd stood behind him. He punched him in the nose, and the guy whirled backward, slamming into the table in the middle of the cabin.

I glanced at Syra. "Can you get this thing started and get us out of here? Declan's got that guy taken care of, and I can undo the ropes."

"On it." She crouched at Donnie's side, searching the dead guy's pockets. His form was already disappearing. Because I'd killed him, he wouldn't return to the underworld like a normal demon.

Donnie the Beater was dead. For good.

She pulled out a set of keys. "Jackpot!"

I jumped onto the dock and hurried to the front of the boat, untying the rope that bound it to the dock. As I moved the ropes on the side, I caught sight of a figure hurrying toward us, confusion on his face.

Crap.

"Hey!" The guy raised a hand over his head, waving. "Hey, you!"

Heart pounding, I sprinted toward the second rope. There were three total.

He picked up the pace, running. I untied the rope.

The engine roared to life.

The guy was getting closer.

"Hurry!" shouted Syra. "That's the owner."

I jumped back onto the boat and ran to the last rope, drawing my sword from the ether. I sliced through it, and the boat's engine roared as it backed out of its slip.

Syra was good, quickly maneuvering the boat around. She kept her head tilted away from the docks and crouched low, probably so the drug lord couldn't identify her.

I stood on the deck, my hair whipping in the wind as I watched the guy stop at the edge of the dock, staring at us in shock. He wore perfectly pressed khakis and a pale blue Polo shirt. He didn't look like a drug dealer. He looked like a human frat boy. Except his eyes were ice cold.

It was a disguise, that was for sure. Something to make him look harmless.

He was anything but harmless. I could feel the dark magic radiating from him. Despair clawed at my chest, followed by pain deep in my bones.

Shit, this was one of the most awful signatures I'd ever felt.

His face turned red as he glared at us. He raised a hand, no doubt to throw magic at us.

Shit.

It would be a big one.

"Hurry!" I shouted at Syra. "He's about to try to hit us with something big."

We weren't even out of the marina yet. A sign stating a five-miles-per-hour speed limit bobbed on a buoy. But Syra gunned it. The boat jumped forward, surging through the water.

The drug lord hurled a blue blast of magic at us. A sonic boom.

Syra had clearly seen it, because the boat's engine roared even louder, and we lurched forward again.

The sonic boom slammed into the water behind us, creating a wave that washed up over the back of the boat.

"Shit!" Syra shrieked. She punched the gas harder.

The water rushed off the back of the boat, and Syra directed us through the narrow passages of the marina, our wake rocking the boats like mad.

We'd be lucky if the ocean cops didn't get us.

I watched the drug lord's form recede into the distance, my heart thundering. I waved at him, grim satisfaction seething through me.

A wail of police sirens tore through the air, and I spotted blue and red lights farther back in the marina.

Shit. Ocean cops *were* a real thing?

I turned toward Syra. "Problem coming!"

Her eyes were already wide, and she pushed a black lever at her right-hand side. The throttle, I thought it was called. The boat jumped forward again, going insanely fast. I clung to the rails as I made my way back toward her.

I stopped near her side. "Can we outrun them?"

She looked behind, spotting the two police boats with flashing red and blue lights. She frowned. "Maybe. Probably. Cop boats are fast. But this baby? It was built to outrun them."

"Good." I grinned as she steered us out onto the open ocean.

"Thank fates the waves are small," she muttered.

Seriously.

She punched up the speed one more time. "This is max speed."

My hair whipped in the wind, snapping against my skin. I peered down into the cabin to see Declan standing there, a dead demon at his feet. He brushed off his hands.

"That the last of them?" I asked.

"Yeah. We got a problem up there?"

I turned around to see the cops still chasing. "Maybe."

He joined us on the deck, staring back at the cops. "Good thing we stole a drug boat. At least we're fast."

"No kidding."

Eventually, we lost the cops. They just couldn't keep up with a boat this fast.

Syra dropped the speed a bit.

"Why'd you do that?" I asked. "We're in a hurry."

She pointed to the gas gauge. "That speed burns about fifty gallons per hour. We won't even make it to Eleuthera with that."

Oh fates. I hadn't thought about running out of gas in the middle of the Bermuda Triangle. "Smart move."

She nodded absentmindedly. Her attention was already taken by the high-tech dials and screens in front of her. She muttered to herself as she fiddled with them.

"Do you know how to get to Eleuthera?" I asked.

"No."

"Um—"

"No one does. We just need to get into the main part of the triangle and find it from there."

"How big is the space?"

She shrugged. "I don't know. But I've heard that people are able to find what they're looking for there. If they're lucky. And worthy."

All right. I could handle that. It wasn't dissimilar from other magical places in that regard. And I trusted Syra. She was doing this to help save Magic's Bend, not for a payment she would skip out with.

The sun beat down as we sped across the brilliant blue ocean. We were nearly out of sight of land when my phone buzzed in my pocket.

I pulled it out, spotting Ana's name before I picked up. "Hello?"

"Aerdeca?"

"Yeah, any luck finding the Oraxia demon?"

"No. I'm sorry. Dead ends every time. I'm not going to be able to find him."

Crap. And all three of my FireSoul friends were turned to stone. I straightened my shoulders and made my voice sound confident. "Thanks. I really appreciate it. We'll figure out a way to find him."

"I'm going to go help with the evacuation. Let me know if you need anything."

"Thanks, Ana." I hung up the phone and looked at Declan. "Ana couldn't find him."

Declan leaned against the boat's front console and frowned. "It's unlikely we'll have time to track him *and* get the potion, so there's only one way to know where he'll show up."

"Monitor the city at the six-hour mark and catch him before he deploys his damned spell."

Declan nodded. "It'll be dangerous, but it's probably our only hope."

I chewed on my lip, thinking. "It's a risk for everyone who is on lookout if we fail. We shouldn't try it until we have the potion to get him to turn back the spell."

"Agreed."

I slumped, exhaustion overtaking me. I'd really been hoping that Ana could find the demon. Hearing the bad news just made our problems that much bigger.

Syra turned to me and squinted. "You look like hell."

"Um, thanks?"

"I just mean tired. Like, really tired."

"Well, I can't remember when I last slept, so..." I shrugged. That pretty much explained it all. "I have a Power-Up Potion for when I really need it."

Syra grimaced. "Hate those things. Fake energy."

"Better than no energy."

"True enough. But we have an hour or two before we reach the triangle. You should go catch some shut-eye down below. I'll holler at you when it starts to get dicey."

Oh, that sounded *divine.*

Even just a thirty-minute nap would be amazing. "You sure?"

"I insist. We need you strong to fight whatever's coming at us in the triangle." She looked at Declan, frowning. "You too. You also look like shit."

Declan cracked a smile. "Kind of you to notice. I put a lot of effort into the look."

I chuckled as I walked by him. "Come on. You've got to be dragging, too."

"A bit." He followed me into the cabin.

The bodies of the demons had disappeared, but blood was splattered here and there. A lot of the furniture was damaged, too, the curtains torn off the little windows.

"Wow, you really had a tussle with that demon."

"Stronger than I expected." The corner of his mouth quirked up in a sexy smile. "A nice challenge though."

I stopped in the middle of the boat's living space and inspected it. The couch was soaked with demon blood, and there was only one bedroom, located at the front of the boat. I could see the big bed through the little door.

Actually, it wasn't that big a bed.

I turned around, looking for a second place to sleep.

There was none.

"I'll take the floor," Declan said.

"That's not necessary. Come on." My heart started to thud as I walked toward the door, wondering if he would follow.

There was the briefest hesitation, but he did.

I didn't bother yanking off my boots. That'd be a bad idea, if this trip was going to be anything like the last one I'd taken with Syra.

I flopped onto the mattress, my head sinking into the pillow. The comfort made it all the more obvious how much my body ached and how tired I was.

Declan lay down next to me, much more gracefully. His shoulder was about two feet from mine, and I couldn't help the tingle of awareness that snaked through me. A shiver ran down my back, and I turned to look at him, unable to help myself.

He was looking right back at me.

"Hey." My voice came out a little rough as memories of our kiss played through my mind.

It had been good. Really good.

I'd never felt chemistry like that before, and it hadn't gone anywhere.

I was exhausted, but suddenly I didn't care. I'd wanted Declan since I'd met him. Wanted him *bad*. His strength seduced me, and his face beguiled me.

I might not be able to trust him, but I liked him.

One minute I was lying on my side of the bed, and the next, I'd rolled over to his.

As if he'd sensed me coming, he rolled to meet me, his hands going around my waist.

Oh fates.

This was happening.

11

Declan gripped my waist, strong and firm, and a shiver of desire went up my spine. He dragged me toward him, pulling my body full against his. Every inch of him was hard muscle, strength born of battle.

Heat exploded inside me.

Fates, how I wanted him.

I moaned low in my throat, unable to help myself, and rubbed my entire body against his. He groaned, a sound that was almost animal, and dipped his head to mine.

His kiss was one of possession, and desire sparked through me. Stars detonated behind my eyelids. Every part of me lit up like a firework, and I pulled him closer to me, wanting to tear off every inch of his clothes.

He knew just how to move, where to provide friction and how much. His hands were strong and confident, sweeping over my body and hitting all the right places. My head swam with pleasure as his mouth moved expertly on mine.

Clothes.

I needed to get out of my clothes.

Right now.

I was going to push him over and strip him naked, then jump on him.

The low noises of pleasure that he made, and the hardness of his body, told me that he thought that would be a pretty good idea, too.

I pushed on his shoulders, ready to put my plan into action, when the boat hit a particularly big wave.

I stiffened.

Shit.

We were on a tiny boat, just feet from Syra. The door wasn't even closed. I'd wanted him so badly I'd forgotten all of that.

I pulled back at the same time he did, my breath heaving.

"Now isn't the time." His voice was rough with regret.

I shivered and lay back.

He was right, damn it.

I wanted this—so badly—but literally any second now, we could face some disaster at sea. We were heading to the Bermuda Triangle, for gods' sake. And Syra could hear us.

And we needed to get some rest if we wanted to be able to fight well. In battles like this, fighting well was the difference between living and dying.

I released a shuddery breath.

He leaned over me, his hand on my stomach.

I looked up at him, feeling closer to him than I ever had before.

Sure, a lot of it was hormones. But they were *convincing* hormones.

The heat faded from his gaze—just a little bit—and something almost like tenderness took its place. "Hey. You're not at all what you seem, are you?"

"I'm exactly what I seem." And that was the truth. The person I presented to him and to the world was real. It was just that there was a secret side to me that I didn't share.

And he was probably picking up on that.

Declan was a smart guy. And with chemistry like ours, it was probably even easier to get a feel for me.

He nodded. "Yeah, actually. I believe that. But it's like there are two of you."

"Split personalities?" I grinned.

"No, they're combined. The fancy ice queen and the badass fighter. I like them both. But there's a lot more to you than you show the world. Your sister sees it, but you try to hide it from everyone else."

"You hardly know me."

"I'm quick. And I feel like I've known you a lot longer than I actually have."

Funny, I felt the same way.

"You're warm with Mordaca, but cold with your friends. Like you put a shield up."

"No, I don't." I totally did that. All the time. It was second nature.

"Don't lie. It's so obvious that a blind person could see it."

"No, it's not, because my friends *don't* see it." I made sure of it. "And you've only seen me with them a couple times. So, what do you know?"

"A lot." He gave me a searching look. "What are you hiding? Does it have anything to do with the secret chamber below your house?" He shook his head. "Scratch that. It definitely has to do with that. Those Aerlig vines are a powerful protective spell. No way they're protecting your weapons collection."

"One, I love my weapons. Of course they could protect them."

"That's true, except for the fact that you store your weapons in the ether." His gaze softened. "Tell me what you're hiding."

"Not hiding anything. And why would you even want to know, anyway?"

"Because I like you. And because it seems like a pretty big burden. Secrets grow and become heavy."

Wasn't that the truth.

From the moment we'd escaped Grimrealm, Mari and I had hidden. First, it was out of a desire to not be recaptured by our family. We'd changed everything about ourselves, and gotten rid of every characteristic we'd had in Grimrealm. They couldn't find us if they didn't recognize us.

Then, we'd hidden our dragon blood because we'd learned just how dark the world really was. Dani, the only person we'd ever trusted with our secret, had turned us over to the Order of the Magica, who had, in turn, used us and our power. If we hadn't escaped, we could have been forced to do truly terrible things.

So yeah, we weren't big on trusting.

The Council of Demon Slayers provided us with a level of protection—as long as we did our deadly jobs. They had their own reasons for secrets, anyway.

Fortunately, I liked danger, so the situation worked out well for me. And I believed in our mission.

True, it meant I had a lot of secrets, but I was used to bearing that burden. It was worth it.

"Fine," I said. "Maybe I'll tell you something. But I want to know your secrets first. You've been real quiet about who you work for. Who hires the fallen angel bounty hunter?"

His jaw tightened just slightly, as if the question made him uncomfortable. Good. I was uncomfortable, too.

He drew in a deep breath, his gaze meeting mine. When he spoke, it was clear he'd never spoken these words aloud before. They sounded like they were being dragged up from the depths of the sea. "I work for the High Court of the Angels."

"The what?"

"Exactly." His gaze was serious. "We never speak of it. Ever."

"What is it?"

"The most powerful angels in the world. In the same way that demons are made from evil given form, the highest angels in the land were made for good given form."

"And what's their role?"

"There are only three of them now, and they cannot walk upon the earth. So bounty hunters like me do their dirty work for them."

"Capturing demons?"

He nodded. "Demons provide valuable information that the High Court can use. It's why they send me after the most dangerous ones."

I nodded, my mind spinning. "Ah, so you aren't so bad. It's not just for the money, is it?"

"No." His hand tightened around my waist. "I've never told anyone that before. I'm not supposed to share it."

"I won't tell anyone." I could definitely understand working for a secret organization. My mind moved back to earlier today. "What was the scene in nightmare alley?"

He hesitated, then forced himself to talk. "Our greatest defeat in the demon wars."

I gaped. "That was real?"

He nodded, his gaze going distant.

"I thought it was your worst fear."

"It was my worst fear. And it came true." Some of the color had faded from his face. "We'd been given the wrong intel about the battle. It should have been a much smaller force, made of a different species of demons. Instead, it was their biggest army. They had weapons we'd never seen before."

"You were uninjured."

"I was injured, just not as badly as the others. I'm a good fighter."

"You're the best fighter. Clearly."

"That day I was." His shoulders sagged a bit. "That day, we lost eighty percent of our force."

Oh fates, he'd lived through such terrible things. My heart ached like a wound. I rubbed his shoulder. "I'm sorry I made you relive that. But thank you for telling me."

He sucked in a slow, deep breath, clearly trying to shake off the memories. "You need a reason to trust me. And clearly, this is a game of you show me yours, and I'll show you mine."

The words were light, but there was still a heaviness to his tone.

I smiled slightly, hoping to get his mind off the memories. "There are better ways to play that game, you know."

A bit more of the sadness faded from his face, replaced by a wolfish smile. "I wouldn't mind playing that sometime."

I hoped it'd be soon.

He didn't say anything. Neither did I.

Clearly, he was waiting for me to show him mine. I would rather have torn off my shirt. Instead, I sucked in a deep breath. I could tell him just a little bit. Not the most dangerous stuff, but enough to get him off my back.

"Swear you won't tell anyone?" I already knew the answer. I could sort the good guys from the bad guys in the same way I could determine if people were telling the truth.

He was a good guy.

His stories said it. Who he was said it. When he'd healed me, the connection had given me insight into who he was.

I could trust him, at least with this little bit of info. He worked for a secret organization, and so did I. We'd keep that secret for each other, and if I told him, he'd trust me more.

"Course not." He smiled gently, as if he understood why I would ask.

And he did. We both had our secrets that we kept from the

world. Two peas in a pod. A very violent pod, given our professions. But a pod, all the same.

"I'm a member of the Council of Demon Slayers."

Understanding lit his eyes. "Of course. It explains why you insist on killing them. And why you didn't like me at first."

"Freaking bounty hunter, always getting in the way and swooping up my catch. I really don't like your kind, you know." I winked. Clearly it was different now that I knew who he worked for.

"But you like me."

"Kinda."

"You told me your secret."

"Yep." I still couldn't believe I'd done it. But it felt good. It had been a burden too long. And it wasn't the big secret anyway. That would require a *lot* more trust. The kind I'd probably never develop.

"But you also use the demon blood in your blood sorcery business, right?"

"I do. Multitasking. And it's good cover."

"Why all the secrecy, though? I know that the Council of Demon Slayers likes to keep their operatives secret. You'd be a target if demons knew you could kill them for good."

"Exactly." It was one of a demon's greatest strengths. Most times, if they were killed on earth, they'd wake up back in their underworld, ready to try again. Like a video game. It made them extra aggressive and bold, since they knew that no death was permanent.

Unless I delivered it.

"Working undercover is one of our main job descriptions. Like a spy," I added. "It's easier to catch them when it's not widely known what I am."

I didn't mention my childhood, or hiding from my family. Or my dragon blood.

He'd never know about those things.

Exhaustion was pulling at me, anyway.

Declan's strong hand closed around mine, and warmth flowed through me.

"There's more to you than all of this," he said. "But thank you for telling me what you do."

"Yeah." Sleep pulled at me.

I drifted off, my mind totally focused on the feeling of Declan's hand around mine.

I slept.

At some point—I don't know when—Syra's voice echoed down the stairs. "Wake up! Trouble's coming!"

I bolted upright, my heart leaping into my throat. Next to me, Declan did the same. We were out of bed a second later, racing up the little stairs to the main deck.

"What's wrong?" I asked.

Declan looked at Syra. "Are we nearly to the triangle?"

"I think so. And we need to be ready." She sniffed the air.

All I could smell was the fresh ocean breeze, but she seemed to be looking for something. Her brow was creased with worry.

The air smelled different in the Bermuda Triangle? Maybe it was the magic.

"There, that's it." She sniffed again. "Smell that?"

Declan sniffed. "It doesn't smell any different."

"You'll sense it later, because it is *definitely* there. Dark magic."

I didn't smell anything either. "What kind of supernatural are you, anyway?"

"Siren." She gestured to the sea around us. "So this is kind of my thing."

"No wonder you can sense danger." Magic prickled lightly against my skin. It didn't hurt, but it didn't feel good either. "I can feel it."

She nodded. "Yeah. Second signature picking up. I smelled it first, but that's what it feels like. We're entering the triangle."

The air seemed to shimmer around us, and I swallowed hard. "I think I see it."

"Yeah, we're fully in it now." She slowed the boat, inspecting our surroundings. "It's huge, so keep your eyes peeled for anything that looks different. Or feels different."

"We're just going to feel our way through?" Declan asked.

"Basically." She shrugged. "I have a knack for the sea. Even the haunted sea. You don't have to worry. Much."

"How many islands are in the Bermuda Triangle?" I searched the horizon for anything out of the ordinary, but I saw nothing except sparkling teal sea and blue sky.

"A lot. No one knows how many. But I've heard of Eleuthera. It's an emerald gem of an island, or so they say. A pirate's island."

"X marks the spot?" Declan asked.

"Exactly." She grinned. "And if anyone can find this island, it's me."

Damn, we were lucky to have found her. Not only was she a skilled captain, she was a siren. Beyond singing and being mistresses of the deep, I didn't know what they were capable of. But her confidence was a comfort.

Overhead, the clouds began to darken. Within seconds, they were swirling ominously overhead.

Syra looked up. "That's not good."

Thunder cracked, but there was no lightning to follow it. The thunder shook my bones, so where was the flash of light? The wind picked up drastically, whipping my hair back from my face. It was so shockingly cold that goose bumps rose on my skin.

"That's not thunder." Syra's face turned white. "You're going to want to hold on. This is going to take some fancy steering."

She turned the boat right, keeping it into the wind.

The clouds were lowering, cutting out the sun. Swirls of dark gray and black surrounded us, cold mist and wind. The ocean turned an iron gray.

My heart thundered in my ears as the weather turned foul.

"What is it?" Declan shouted over the roar of the thunder.

"An angry wind god!" Syra squinted into the darkness ahead of us. "Hang on!"

She maneuvered expertly, keeping the front of the boat facing the storm. "We're almost out of it!"

But the winds changed faster than the boat could accommodate. They caught us from the side, lifting the boat into the air.

I clung to the railing. "What the hell is happening?"

The winds raised us high over the ocean surface, buffeting us about. This shouldn't be possible. The boat rose on the wind, ten feet up. Twenty feet. Thirty feet above sea level.

We rocked and pitched, as if we were a toy clutched in the hand of an angry god.

Fear iced my skin.

We are in trouble.

Nerves chilling my skin. "This isn't how physics works!"

"It's how the wind god works, and he's got us now!" Syra looked around the boat, eyes sharp and clever. "We should have stolen a sailboat."

"We need a sail?" Declan asked.

"Yeah." Her face brightened. "Go check the cabin. Get the biggest bed sheet you can find. No—get the blanket. The sheet will be too thin for this wind."

Declan stumbled into the cabin, fighting the rocking of the wind.

"What else do you need?" I shouted.

"Rope! And that angel is gonna have to fly."

"On it." I clung to the railing as the wind threatened to catch me. The boat pitched in midair as I scrambled toward the rope that was tied off to the back of the boat.

I crouched low, wrapping an arm around the railing as I called a dagger from the ether and cut the rope off from where it was tied.

I surged upright, finding Syra moving away from the wheel. She'd given up trying to keep us on course. The rudder was way too small to catch the wind.

Declan appeared in the doorway to the cabin, a big white quilt in his hands. "Will this do?"

"Yeah!" Swiftly, Syra untied another rope from the side of the boat. "Bring it here."

Declan handed her the blanket. She cut two holes in the bottom corners and threaded the ropes through, then tied them off.

I hung onto the boat as I watched, nearly blasted overboard by the wind.

Finished, she looked up at us. "This idea is insane, but it's all I've got." She held up both ropes. "There's no mast on a speedboat, but we still need a sail to catch the wind and drive us back down to the ocean surface. So we're going to tie off the bottom corners of this blanket to the middle of the boat." She pointed at Declan. "Then you, angel boy, are going to fly the top half of this blanket up into the air."

She had a crazed look in her eyes, as if she knew how insane this was but didn't care.

"Then we have a crappy sail," I said. "And we just need to catch the right gust of wind."

She pointed at me. "Exactly."

"This is insane," Declan said.

"*This* is the Bermuda Triangle." Syra grinned, clearly unafraid of death. "And if you believe in a higher power, I'd suggest praying. Because yeah, this is nuts."

I grabbed one of the ropes that was tied to a corner of the blanket. "Where's the best spot?"

Syra pointed to the right side of the boat, roughly halfway between the front and the back. "Tie it off around there. I'll do the other side. And you, angel boy, get ready to fly."

Declan saluted.

I moved forward on the deck, keeping low to the ground and making sure that I was always holding on to something sturdy. I found a silver metal fixture—a cleat, I thought it was called—and tied off the rope. Syra did the other side.

I turned to Declan, whose wings flared at his back, dark and gleaming. He grabbed the blanket, and flew up about ten feet, as far as he could. It was clearly a struggle to fly against the wind, but he managed to make a sail.

Unfortunately, the wind didn't catch it. At least, not in the direction we needed.

"Come on!" Syra shouted. "We need our weight at the front of the boat to help point us downward."

I scrambled around the side of the quilt and crawled to the bow. *Please let this work.*

She and I didn't weigh all that much combined. Not compared to the speedboat. We positioned ourselves at the very front, where it terminated in a sharp point, and I felt the boat dip just slightly.

My heart thundered in my ears as the wind tore at my hair.

In the air, Declan struggled against the wind, trying to get the sail to catch it in a way that would send us back toward the ocean surface.

This is the most insane, impossible thing I've ever done.

And it wasn't working.

12

No matter what we did, the wind just wouldn't cooperate.
Crap.

Fear and icy wind chilled me to my bones.

If we failed, Magic's Bend was screwed.

There was only one thing to do. I didn't hesitate, just lowered my hand by my side, where Syra couldn't see it. Quickly, I sliced by finger with my nail. Blood welled.

I called upon my magic, upon the gift of my dragon's blood. I imagined controlling the wind, molding it to my will. At first, nothing happened. I tried harder, pushing my magic outward. It swelled on the air, and even I could feel it. The sound of birds chirping. My signature.

Syra looked at me, confused. "What are you doing?"

I ignored her. It took everything I had to get ahold of the wind—and even then, I could only control a bit of it.

I envisioned a column of wind shooting at the sail from exactly the right angle, driving us downward. I was behind the sail, so I couldn't see if the clouds looked different, but eventually, the white blanket bulged toward us, wind filling it.

The boat began to lower toward the water's surface.

"That's it! Keep going!" Syra shouted.

I didn't know if she was talking to me or Declan, but I kept up the effort, trying to drive the wind into the sail. It slowed a bit, weakening, and I squeezed my eyes shut, concentrating. Blood dripped from my finger to cover my hand, and the more I bled, the stronger the magic was.

It was screwed up, really.

But it was working. When I peeked my eyes open, we were nearly to the surface of the water.

"Come on!" Syra shouted. "We need to get the bow up. Go to the back!"

I scrambled after her, my white blood dripping on the white deck as I followed her. I didn't give up on the wind, though, sending it right into the sail. Declan was still aloft, struggling against the breeze.

Syra and I crouched at the back of the boat. Our weight barely did anything, so I tried to change the wind's direction. I didn't want it blowing quite so hard downward anymore.

The boat leveled out, finally hitting the water with a hard splash. I let go of my magic, letting it fade. My signature disappeared from the air.

Syra leapt for the steering wheel and pushed up on the throttle so the engine roared. She steered us into the wind, gunning it away from the storm.

The wind seemed to have lessened some, as if the wind god had given up. Declan landed on the deck, and I hurried toward him and grabbed the white blanket to wipe my blood away. The liquid blended with the fabric.

"Are you all right?" I shouted.

"Yeah. We got lucky there." But he gave me a searching look, as if he almost didn't believe the words.

"Totally lucky!" I turned from him, checking on Syra.

Her face was *slightly* more relaxed now, though that didn't say much. She met my gaze and shouted, "We're almost out of it!"

"Thank fates." I joined her.

Within a few minutes, the wind had dropped to a breeze. I collapsed into the chair next to Syra's, which she never used. "Quick thinking there."

"I'm just glad we made it out." She stared straight ahead, navigating us across the sparkling blue water.

"Without the wind, this place is paradise." Declan leaned over the rail and looked down into the water.

"That's the thing about paradise," Syra said. "When it goes bad, it goes *bad.*"

The sea was flat and the breeze light as Syra headed toward the horizon. Occasionally, she looked at the fancy navigation equipment and modified her course.

I caught her eye. "I thought you said you didn't know where you were going?"

"I don't, not exactly. But I'm setting a course due west-north-west, which is roughly where Eleuthera is supposed to be. As we get closer, there will hopefully be clues to get us right on the dot."

I turned to search the sea around us. "What kind of clues?"

"That kind." She pointed straight ahead, and I spun to look.

Two massive pillars of rock rose out of the ocean. They were like little mountains with a channel of water between them.

"Should we go around them?" I asked.

"Can't. I've heard of these before." She looked around the deck. "Can you find us some line? Really long. Way longer than what we used for the sail. Look inside the hatches at the bow and stern."

"Sure." I headed to the bow while Declan went to the stern.

She slowed as we approached the jagged little mountains.

I crouched at the hatch and pulled on the steel ring, lifting up the white plastic door. A coiled rope lay within. "Jackpot."

I pulled it out and hurried back to Syra. Declan had a similar rope gripped in his hand.

"What's coming?" Declan asked.

"Whirlpool." The seriousness of Syra's voice made me swallow hard.

"Whirlpool?" Holy fates.

"Big one. Be ready to tie the lines off to one of those cleats." She pointed to the metal fixtures at the side of the boat, right in the middle. "I'll tell you when. And brace yourselves."

I watched the small mountains approach as Syra steered us toward the gap between them. The air seemed to sparkle with magic and menace.

I shared a quick glance with Declan, then looked back.

The rock cliffs rose high on either side as we entered the channel. Smaller peaks of rock rose up from them like tiny mountains.

The water ahead of us was flat and calm, but there was an ominous feeling to the air. A heaviness that indicated there was a spell waiting for us.

Magic sparked across my skin, sharp and fierce. The water in front of us began to move, small waves forming.

"Here it comes." Syra's face set in serious lines as she leaned forward, her hands never leaving the wheel. "We need to see what direction it goes before we tie off the lines."

The water began to spin, moving in a counter-clockwise direction. Syra turned hard on the wheel, directing us toward the right, but the water pulled even harder.

The front of the boat was dragged to the left, and the whirlpool caught our boat. Water splashed and wind roared as the whirlpool picked up speed, dragging us along.

My heart thundered as the whirlpool deepened in the middle.

It was just going to keep growing, becoming bigger and deeper, until we were sucked into the ocean depths.

Syra pointed to the right side of the boat. "Tie your ropes to the cleats on that side. Then you need to fly them to the cliff on the right and tie them off."

"Then we drag ourselves out," I guessed.

"I hope you're strong."

Thankfully I was, but we were moving *fast.* Round and round, the whirlpool pulled harder and deeper.

Declan and I hurried to the cleats, keeping our center of balance low. If I fell off now...

As much as I loved swimming, I wasn't super into *dying while swimming.*

Declan and I struggled to tie our ropes off to the cleats at the edge of the boat, which were about ten feet apart. Once my rope was secure, I handed the loose end to him.

"Hold on tight." His wings flared wide behind his back, black and bright.

He launched himself into the air, the ropes dangling down below him.

"Damn, that's cool." Syra's voice was strained from the effort of trying to keep the wheel turned hard to the right. If the rudders failed, we might be driven faster into the middle of the whirlpool.

My heart pounded as the water roared in circles, dragging us along. We were gradually moving deeper into the whirlpool as it widened, the boat starting to keel over as my world began to go vertical.

Fear iced my skin as I clung to one of the ropes that was tied off to the boat and watched Declan. He flew the ropes over to the jagged cliff face. They could barely reach, and he had to time it just right so he tied them off when the boat was on the closest side of the whirlpool. Only then were they long enough.

Come on, come on.

He looped the first one around a huge pinnacle of rock that didn't have any sharp edges, and quickly tied it off. The rope pulled taut, and the boat stopped, jerking abruptly. The force threw me to the side, and I grabbed the taut rope to steady myself. Then I began to pull.

Declan had tied off the rope that was closer to the stern, and the bow began to tip farther into the water. We were now nearly vertical, the whirlpool opening up like a huge monster's mouth.

As I pulled, I looked over my shoulder, staring down into the black pit, dark magic bellowing up from the depths.

My stomach heaved, and I turned back to the rope, yanking hard.

"Hurry!" Syra screamed.

Quickly, Declan tied off the other rope, and the front of the boat straightened out. We were still nearly vertical, but at least there wasn't so much pressure on one cleat. I didn't want it to tear right off the boat.

I pulled on my rope as hard as I could, trying to drag us out of the whirlpool. My muscles strained, and sweat popped out on my brow.

In seconds, Declan was back on the boat and folding his wings into his body. He bent to his rope and grabbed it, pulling hard.

Together, we inched our way out of the whirlpool, which roared and splashed, the water moving so fast that if I fell off, I'd be lost in seconds.

"Almost there!" Syra shouted.

Every muscle in my body screamed with the strain, and the whirlpool increased its speed and pull, as if it sensed that we were getting away. We were nearly halfway out of the whirlpool, but it felt like there was so much left to go.

"Just a little farther," Declan grunted.

I gave it everything I had, my skin chilled with fear. The whirlpool gaped behind us, threatening to drag us down into the deep.

Finally, we reached flat water.

"Cut the ropes!" Syra yelled, revving the engine.

I drew a knife from the ether and sliced through the rope. Declan did the same. As soon as we were free, Syra pushed up on the throttle, and the engine roared. The boat leapt forward, gaining traction and speeding away from the whirlpool.

Panting, I turned to watch it disappear into the distance. The water seemed to roar its frustration, the wind loud and fierce as it closed back up.

I sagged onto the deck, my muscles sore. "Holy fates, that was hard."

"Nicely done!" Syra cried.

I looked up at her and smiled.

Declan rubbed my shoulder. "Well done."

"Thanks. You too. That was some fancy flying."

"Kind of my specialty." He gave a wry smile. "Want a back rub?"

"I'd think that's a lame pickup line, but my shoulders are killing me and I bet yours are too."

"Why can't it be both?"

I laughed, liking him more and more. After what had happened in the cabin earlier, I was up for more of him, any time I could get it. "Okay."

Might as well take the good things while I could get them, right? Who knew what we'd be up against next? And time was weighing on me heavily. Soon, a fifth district would go down. Leaving us with just six more hours. Would the Protectorate find a nullifier in time? Declan's people hadn't gotten back to him yet. Not to mention, if we couldn't use a transportation charm to get out of the Bermuda Triangle, we'd be too slow to make it back.

I shook away the dark thoughts and turned my back toward Declan. His fingers dug into the sore spots on my shoulders, and I tried to focus only on that.

I groaned and leaned back, pleasure surging through me. Memories of what had happened earlier amped up the tension. "Wow, you're a professional."

His hands moved like magic over my skin, and it took everything I had not to melt into a boneless puddle. Heat began to rise within me, bringing with it an intense desire to turn around and kiss him. My lips tingled with it.

But Syra was here. And we were going to be fighting something else any minute, I was sure of it.

So I just focused on the back rub, letting him work away the soreness in my muscles so I'd be ready to use them again soon. The warm sun beat down, and the ocean sparkled a beautiful, impossible blue.

It was amazingly nice.

"I need a vacation," I said. "Something like this, but with fewer chances of dying a horrible death."

"Couldn't agree more," Declan said.

After a while, I looked back at him. "Your turn."

He cocked a smile. "Not going to turn that down."

We switched places, and I got to work on his shoulders. Damn, he had nice shoulders. Perfectly muscled and warm from the sun. A low moan of appreciation rumbled through him, and I vowed he'd make that sound again.

This was fun. I could spend all day touching him, and I enjoyed every second of the back rub, way more than was probably normal. Or maybe it was a perfectly normal amount, considering he was a hot-as-hell fallen angel that I wanted to jump on.

No. Bad.

Now was *not* the time.

Not only were we in the freaking Bermuda Triangle, this spot wasn't even close to private.

"You did something with the wind earlier, didn't you?" he asked.

I stiffened, my hands stilling on his shoulders. Quickly, I moved them again, not wanting him to notice that I was acting weird.

"The plan with the sail wasn't working. It wasn't *going* to work. The wind never would have caught it. Then I felt your magic swell, and the wind came."

Shit, in my stress I hadn't hidden it enough. I'd also been pouring so much magic into it that I probably wouldn't have been *able* to control my signature.

That was why I tried to stick to only creating small magic with my dragon blood.

Once I tried to do the big, complicated stuff, it was way too easy for people to notice. They'd definitely notice if I tried to ever make permanent magic—that would almost kill me.

"I don't know what you're talking about," I said.

"You keep using new magic. Things I've never seen you do before. That's unusual. No one can make new magic."

"It's your imagination." I tried to laugh, to turn this conversation into a funny misunderstanding.

But my laugh sounded strangled.

"There's more to you than you show the world, Aerdeca." He repeated the words from earlier, speaking so quietly that Syra wouldn't be able to hear. "You trusted me with your demon-slaying secret. You can trust me with this, too."

Was he guessing what I was?

My skin chilled.

No.

That was too dangerous.

He trusted me, but once he found out that I was a Dragon Blood and that I could create enough magic to destroy the world? No one trusted that kind of Magica. We were too scary. I'd seen how the FireSouls were mistrusted and abused when people knew how powerful they were. Not to mention how we'd been treated.

It was one thing to tell him the demon slayer secret. That wasn't that big a deal.

But this?

This was huge.

It was too big a secret to reveal.

"I'll stop prying," Declan said. "But I'm here if you want to tell me."

A chill went over me. Not a bad one. More like a subtle *knowing.*

Like my soul believed Declan. Like it knew he was special. Trustworthy.

That was just crazy, though. Actually crazy.

"Hey, guys, something is coming."

Thank fates. A distraction. With any luck, he'd forget about this.

Ha. As if.

I let go of Declan and stood, searching the sea. She pointed toward a dark shadow on the water. It was long and narrow, snaking through the waves.

"What is it?" I asked.

"Don't know, but it's not right." She tried to steer around it, but it only grew, stretching longer. She leaned forward and squinted. "Sargassum."

"*Sargassum natans* or *Sargassum fluitans*?"

"Both, actually."

Ooh, nice. I liked that she knew her classifications.

"What?" Declan asked.

"Those are the two species of Sargassum most commonly found in the Caribbean. I wondered which it was."

"Can you smell the stink of dark magic in the air?"

I sniffed, getting a hint of rotten seaweed that was more than just natural decay.

"At least it's not a giant snake," I said.

Syra shook her head. "I'd almost prefer a snake. This stuff can drag your boat under."

Shit.

In the distance, beyond the weeds, I spotted a pinprick of green against the horizon. I pointed to it. "Is that Eleuthera?"

"I think so," Syra said. "We're going to have to try to go through the weeds. Hang on tight."

She pushed up on the throttle, and the boat surged forward. We were going to try to speed through. I held on as she pushed the boat to its limit. As we neared the long line of seaweed that floated on the surface, the stench of dark magic grew until it was nearly overpowering.

I held my breath as we got closer.

The boat cut across, gliding over the top of the weeds. They were brown and rancid.

I turned around to watch the seaweed disappear behind us. "That wasn't so bad."

The weeds started to snake toward us, racing behind.

Shit.

"Faster," Declan shouted. "It's gaining."

"This is as fast as we go." Syra cursed and looked back. "It's coming for the prop."

As soon as the words left her mouth, the long column of seaweed reached us and wrapped around the propeller. Syra cranked down on the throttle immediately. Probably so she didn't burn out the engine.

"It's going to drag us down!" she shouted.

I drew a long dagger from the ether. "I'm going in."

"Wait!" Syra screamed. She lunged for me, a rope in her hand, and tied it around my waist. "It's strong."

"I'm going with her." Declan drew a sword.

"No." Syra shoved the rope at him. "You gotta pull her back up. I'm not strong enough. Not against that stuff."

The back of the boat began to dip into the water as the weeds pulled us down. I jumped off the boat, my heart in my throat.

Dark water closed around my head, as if the magic in the weeds had polluted the water. All around, the seaweed waved. Then it reached for me, wrapping around my limbs.

In the distance, dark shadows circled.

Immediately, I recognized them.

Sharks.

Oh, shit.

13

P anic clawed at my throat as the seaweed wrapped around my limbs. I ignored the sharks, which were still circling, and hacked at the weeds with my blade, sawing it away from my arms and legs. Then I kicked toward the propeller, which was totally entangled. The weeds pulled taut as they dragged the boat toward the bottom.

I clung to the main column of weeds, sawing away at them. Piece by piece, they fell away from the propeller. My lungs burned, and I kept an eye out for the sharks.

Galeocerdo cuvier. Carcharhinus leucas.

I repeated the scientific names to myself, a calming litany that helped me focus on my task as my lungs burned and my skin chilled with fear. The back of the boat was dipping farther and farther into the water as the weeds pulled downward. More of the bright white hull submerged. The bow might even be pointing out of the water by now.

How long did I have before the boat was destroyed? Before I ran out of air?

As I worked, the weeds twined around my limbs. For every

strand that I hacked away from the propeller, a new one twined around my body.

Declan had better have a good grip on that rope.

I sawed away, my chest aching.

Nearly there. The prop was almost free.

The sharks continued to circle, closer and closer.

They were just curious. Humans weren't the natural prey of sharks, so I was safe.

Mostly.

While that was all true, I knew I'd still make a tasty nibble if a shark decided to add some variety to its diet.

Finally, I sawed away the last of the weeds that twined around the prop. The boat popped upward, the bow smashing onto the surface of the water with a loud crash.

Suddenly, the weeds yanked me down. *Hard.*

The boat had been heavy, but I wasn't. Now that they didn't have to contend with the vessel's weight, the weeds could yank me to the bottom in a heartbeat.

Unable to help myself, I screamed, bubbles escaping my mouth. I thrashed, trying to hack my way free. Deeper and deeper, the weeds dragged me, the water growing darker. So dark I couldn't even see the shadows of the sharks, but I could feel them.

Not a threat, not a threat.

Galeocerdo cuvier. Carcharhinus leucas.

The rope around my waist yanked hard, reminding me that it was there. Pain flared as it dug into the bottom of my ribs.

Declan!

The rope cut in harder. He must be pulling with all his strength.

But the weeds were pulling, too, dragging at my legs. I ached; my lungs burned.

They were evenly matched. Declan and the weeds were equally strong.

Holy fates, they could tear me apart.

Because of the way the rope pulled at me, I couldn't bend over to hack at the weeds. I stashed my dagger in the ether and called upon a sword, the longest one I had.

I reached down and hacked at the weeds that twined around my legs. Black spots danced at the corners of my vision.

Panic blasted through me.

I was about to black out.

I called on every bit of strength I had, finally managing to hack away at the rest of the weeds.

Immediately, I surged upward, water dragging around me. Declan pulled me up so fast that my head burst through the water seconds later. Choking and sputtering, I gasped for air.

Strong hands grabbed my arms and yanked me out of the water.

"Go!" Declan shouted.

Syra gunned it, and water sprayed up from behind the boat as it sped away.

Declan carried me into the cockpit. I coughed and gasped, clinging to him.

"Badass!" Syra said.

"Thanks." I could barely speak. My lungs still burned.

"Are you okay?" Declan's concerned gaze met mine.

"Fine." I sucked in a few more breaths, finally able to speak. "I never thought that seaweed would be one of the scariest things I'd ever face."

Memories of the weeds twisting around me made a shiver run through me.

"I don't see any more around us," Syra said.

Thank fates.

I staggered to my feet, giving Declan's arm an appreciative

squeeze, and joined Syra near the wheel. She was staring out over the blue sea, her gaze glued to the green island in the distance.

"I think that's it," she said. "We just need to find a safe place to leave the boat."

"Who lives there?" Declan asked.

"No humans. Mostly magical creatures and regular animals. And pirate ghosts."

"Ghosts?"

"Yeah. The pirates were killed off by the locals."

"Unfriendly, huh?" Declan asked.

"Nope. Not really. There's danger there, don't get me wrong. But it was the pirates who were unfriendly. Thieves and rapists, pillagers and murderers. From what I've heard, their ship got stuck on the reefs a few hundred years ago. They were given a chance to live nicely with the locals, but they were assholes. So the locals took care of them."

"Wow. Tough locals." I spotted a head pop out of the water in the distance. We were close enough to the island that the figure could have swum from shore. I pointed. "Who's that?"

"One of those same locals I was telling you about." Syra grinned and waved, slowing the boat.

I grabbed a pair of binoculars to get a better look. A beautiful woman was smiling at the boat, her hair slicked back from her face and a triple strand of pearls around her neck.

"A mermaid?" I asked.

"Siren."

"Like you."

"Yeah." A radiant smile spread across Syra's face.

"So the locals who killed the pirates were a group of sirens?" Declan asked.

"Yep. It's mostly women on the island, and they didn't take

kindly to a bunch of seventeenth century men who never bathed and also thought women were chattel."

Declan nodded as if he approved. "So they gave them a chance, and when they proved to be the murderers and rapists that pirates are famous for being, they showed them who was boss."

"Pretty much. It's wild out here. Only the strongest survive." Syra slowed the boat alongside the siren.

I leaned toward Declan. "Well, that's pretty much my favorite story ever."

He grinned. "I can see why. You're bloodthirsty."

"Yep." I joined Syra, who was crouched on the side of the boat to get more level with the siren.

Declan joined us.

The siren was beautiful, with glittering dark eyes and full lips. The sun gleamed on her brown skin, giving her a nearly heavenly glow. Her hair was swept back from her head, drifting in the sea.

"Greetings, sister." Syra reached out and held her hand in a relaxed high-five gesture.

The siren touched her fingertips to Syra's, lining their hands up. Her other hand disappeared beneath the water, then returned, clutching a shell. She held it to her mouth to speak.

"Greetings, sister. I am Elora. Who are your friends?"

"This is Aerdeca, and this is Declan. They're on an important mission to save my town on land." Syra turned to us. "Elora is speaking through the shell as a courtesy to me. I am half siren, so my voice cannot compel you. As a full siren, Elora could make you her slave. But she won't."

Elora nodded. "She is correct."

"Thank you." Declan inclined his head.

Someone who didn't know Declan might say that he was being

more polite because he knew that Elora belonged to a race of women who'd killed off a crew of evil pirates, but I knew it wasn't the case. He was cool and respectful by nature. This particular group of pirates could have learned from him. Don't be a dick, don't get killed.

"Thanks," I said.

She met my gaze. "What are you looking for here?"

I quickly explained about the Oraxia demon and our friends, finishing with the story of the potion that could compel the Oraxia demon to undo the evil spell he'd cast.

"And the Devyver told you that this ingredient you need—the sea sapphire--would be in a cave here on our island?"

"Yes. In the pirate's cave."

She pursed her lips and nodded. "This makes sense. They have many things in that cave. They're ghosts now, by the way."

"I heard the story." Declan smiled.

She nodded. "After the things they tried to do to us, they deserve their fate. They cannot leave their cave, and we cannot enter it. We don't want to, anyway."

"Not even for the gold?" I asked. I wouldn't hate to check out a cave full of gold.

She wrinkled her nose. "No. Ugly stuff. We prefer jewels of the sea." She petted the pearls at her throat, which really were beautiful.

"Can you tell us how to get to the cave?" I asked.

"And if the pirate ghosts have any weaknesses?" Declan added.

"Yes, I'd be happy to." A cunning glint entered her eyes. "I quite like the idea of you annoying the pirates."

"Oh, *happy* to do it." I grinned. "And thanks."

Her face fell. "The only downside is they don't have many weaknesses in their current forms. They cannot be hurt because they are entirely incorporeal. And their touch is deadly."

"How deadly?" Declan asked.

"It will suck the life from you within seconds."

"Shit." I wracked my brain. "So we can't hurt them, but they can kill us with a touch."

Elora nodded. "If they get a grip on you for a few seconds, yes."

"So we'll have to be clever," Declan said.

"*Very* clever." Elora's gaze traveled between us. "I can take you to the cave."

"Thanks." I inclined my head. "I can't even tell you what a big hurry we're in."

"It's my pleasure."

"Can we transport off the island using a transport charm?" Declan asked.

I held my breath, saying a prayer to every god I'd never believed in.

"Yes. You just can't find it using one. Now come on." She gestured to us to follow, then turned and cut through the water, swimming quickly.

Relief relaxed my shoulders. We could get out of here in time, if we were lucky. I looked up at Syra. "You really were the best captain for the job. You've got all the connections."

She shrugged, a quick smile slicing across her face. "What can I say? I'm the best."

Syra returned to the wheel and cranked the engine. Elora swam ahead, and we followed at a safe distance.

I joined Syra at the wheel. "What are you going to do? Can you make it back to the mainland with the gas you have?"

"Possibly, but not probably."

"Come with us, then."

"To the deadly ghost pirate cave?"

"Yeah. We'll all transport out of here when it's done."

She shrugged. "Sure, sounds fun. I like a good ghost battle."

"We're going to need a plan," Declan said. "It doesn't sound like we can fight them outright."

My mind raced as we headed toward the island, searching for ideas. We needed a way to sneak in and get past the ghosts. But that would probably be pretty hard if they were all hiding out in the same place.

Then an idea popped into my head. I turned to my friends. "I've got a plan."

Syra grinned. "Yeah?"

"Yeah. You got a phone with battery?"

"Sure do."

"Fantastic." I laid out my idea.

At first, Declan looked skeptical, but Syra loved it from the get-go.

"I think this has real potential." She nodded, her gaze distant, as if she were imagining it. "Let's do it."

"If we can arrange it," Declan said.

"Oh, we'll make it work." Syra nodded. "I have just the thing."

I moved toward the back of the boat and pressed my fingertips to my comms charm. "Mari?"

"Yeah?" Her voice was quiet.

"Any luck with the nullifier?" Hope made me hold my breath.

"Not yet." She was trying to make her tone hopeful—I could hear it in her voice.

But it sounded fake.

We were down to six hours now. Our odds were getting worse every second.

"Thanks. Which district went down?"

"He just got Darklane."

My heart stuttered.

My neighborhood.

The bastard had frozen my neighborhood.

It'd already been personal, but this made it even worse. I was going to get that son of a bitch.

"It's all total shit," Mari said. "He got a huge proportion of the population, since those stubborn bastards wouldn't leave."

"That just leaves the Historic District, then. And we're running out of time." Not only would we lose our friends, we might never figure out who was behind this.

"The last gap was seven hours, so he's weakening a bit. Taking longer to recoup his magic."

Good. We might need the extra time. We weren't even *on* Eleuthera yet, and we only had about six hours until the final battle.

"Thanks, Mari. We'll be back in time, I promise."

"You better. Safe hunting."

"Safe hunting." I cut the connection.

Declan joined me. "What's the word?"

I told him what Mari had said.

He frowned. "I still haven't heard back about a nullifier either."

Cold sweat dripped down my spine.

As if he could read my fear, he reached out a comforting hand and squeezed my shoulder. "We'll make it work. It'll be okay."

I swallowed hard and nodded, then went to watch Elora swimming in front of the boat.

The siren led us toward a wide cove where the sea glittered an impossible turquoise. The long beach glinted pink in the sun, the fine sand as beautiful as the interior of a conch shell. What a perfect vacation spot. I returned to the cockpit.

"I say we beach this bad boy," Syra said. "Let the sirens play with it."

"I like how you think." The sun had only just dried me off,

and I didn't want to spend the rest of the day wet. *Especially* with squelchy boots that might alert the pirates to our presence.

Ahead of us, Elora climbed out onto the shore. Though she was far away, it was obvious that she was buck naked and looked like a supermodel. She strode toward a rock and grabbed a short, sparkling purple dress that looked like it was made of stars, then tugged it over her head.

Syra slowed the engine and headed toward shore, beaching the boat on the sand.

"That boat is quite nice," Elora said.

"All yours." Syra grinned. "But if you find some white powder in it, just throw it out."

I choked on a laugh.

Elora looked at us, her head tilted and confusion on her face.

"Really," Declan said. "Just bury it on the island. It's poison."

Elora's eyes widened, and she nodded. "All right."

We climbed off the boat, and my feet sank into the firm pink sand.

Oh, this is lovely.

I thought it but didn't say it—didn't really fit my ice queen persona.

"I'd rather be swimming than tricking pirates," Syra said. "Though, actually, on second thought, given our plan..."

I looked at her, catching sight of the sparkle in her eyes. I headed up the beach, following after Elora. Declan joined us.

At the tree line—which consisted primarily of tall pine trees of a variety I didn't recognize—Elora turned back to us. "It's not far through the trees. The cave's entrance is on land."

She led us on a winding path through the towering trees. They were slender and finely needled, allowing the sun to shine through. Eventually, the sandy path disappeared, and we were trekking through the wilderness.

"You weren't kidding when you said that you rarely came here," I said.

She grinned over her shoulder. "There's another name for Pirate's Cave." She lowered her voice to a creepier octave. "Spider Cave."

"Ah, shit." I scowled.

"They're spider crabs, but that really doesn't make them any better," she said.

"From the superfamily *Majoidea*?" I asked.

"I'm not sure what that is," Elora said.

No, a siren would have no need for the human classifications of species. They had their own. "They're a type of long-legged crab."

"Ah, no. They are more like spiders. Half spider, half crab. Twice as creepy."

Yikes. "My favorite." My tone was dry, and Declan chuckled.

A few minutes later, Elora slowed. "We're here. I can take you through the first part of the cave—with the spiders—but once we reach the pirate's domain, I can go no farther."

I caught her eye. "Thank you. Truly."

She nodded, then turned and picked her way through the rocks, finding a hole that led into the ground. We followed her down the sloping rock into the earth.

Immediately, the air was cooler and darker—but almost suffocating. Elora raised her hand, shining a bright glow from her palm.

It illuminated the interior of the long cave, shining upon delicate rock formations and draping spiderwebs. I shivered, a chill racing over me.

"Now, the thing about spider crabs is that they are huge, and their bite is venomous," Elora said. "They are fast, too. Faster than lightning. So if one lands on you, don't fight back. Just freeze. Don't move a single muscle."

Oh fates.

This sounded like hell.

"I mean it," she repeated. "If you move, they will bite you. And the poison will paralyze for hours. Maybe weeks, days, or years. It depends upon the age of the spider."

I drew in a shuddering breath, keeping my voice quiet. "Gotcha. No moving if a spider crab jumps on me."

"How big are they exactly?" Syra asked.

"About the size of turtles."

"Freshwater or sea turtles?" I asked. Because there was a *big* difference between those two.

"Sea turtles."

Oh fates. Those were *big.*

Elora carefully picked her way around a rock formation that jutted out of the ground. "But they are light. So slender that they hardly weigh anything at all."

That really didn't make it sound any better.

I dragged my mind away from the thought of them and focused on following Declan's footsteps, perfectly and silently. He followed Elora, and since he was stepping where she was stepping, I knew it was safe ground. I wasn't going to give a spider a chance to figure out that I was here.

Fortunately, Syra was an excellent cat burglar. I couldn't hear a peep from her behind me. Not a sound of breath or the scuff of a shoe. I'd already known that Declan was a silent hunter. It was something I respected.

The cave wound deeper into the ground, a work of art made of beautifully intricate stone formations. Moss and spiderwebs hung down from the ceiling, and in many places, the ground above was broken away. Sunlight streamed through, giving the whole place an enchanted feel.

Enchanted, but creepy.

Something flashed in front of my face, so fast that I couldn't make a sound. The spider crab was on Declan's back before I could stop.

"Stop!" Elora whispered.

Declan had already frozen. I stared in horror at the massive spider that clung to his back. It really did look like a spider/crab combo, but ghostly as well. The shell gleamed a faint blue with an iridescent sheen.

I caught sight of beady eyes and gleaming fangs. My stomach lurched and my skin chilled.

Ooh, boy. That was definitely different than the aquatic members of the *Majoidea* superfamily.

Declan held perfectly still, and the spider inspected him.

A weight hit my back, and I nearly shrieked. Years of training, of silently hunting demons, was the only thing that kept me quiet. I stiffened, straight as a board, and stared straight ahead, frozen in horror.

I could feel all eight legs, each one clinging around my shoulders and waist. But I couldn't see it. Not as long as I kept my head completely still.

My heart pounded so hard I was sure it was shaking my body. The spider would get pissed any minute and bite.

Oh fates, I wished I didn't have a perfect view of the monster on Declan's back. My eyes were glued to its fangs.

Don't move, don't move, don't move.

"Stay perfectly still," Elora said.

Like in *Jurassic Park.*

The inane thought flashed in my head.

Hell, I'd rather be facing off with a T. rex right now. At least then I could fight.

Elora walked toward us, slow and calm. She opened her mouth and began to sing, this time, without the shell held in front of her face. It was the most beautiful sound I'd ever heard —clear and pure.

On my back, the spider stiffened.

I held perfectly still, my lungs burning from holding my breath. I hadn't drawn in air since the thing had landed on me, and I was growing desperate.

The spider began to move, its feet trailing down my body. Off my shoulders, to my waist, then my hips. Finally, my legs and feet. And it was off, crawling toward the wall.

I sucked in a massive breath.

Declan's spider crawled off him also, and his shoulders sagged.

"Holy fates, that was terrifying," Syra said from behind me.

I turned to her, my pulse still thundering in my ears and my limbs weak from adrenaline. "You had one on you, too?"

She shook her head. "It was scary enough just watching yours."

"Yeah, sure." I'd be having nightmares for months.

"Come on," Elora said. "The downside of singing that song is that the other spiders come to hear it."

Oh, shit.

She picked up the pace, hurrying through the cave. We kept up with her, following right in her footsteps. Scuttling noises came from all around, and I caught sight of skinny figures in the shadows.

I squinted toward them.

Spider crabs, staring out at us from all sides. Eyes gleaming, fangs dripping with poison.

Every muscle in my body couldn't decide if it wanted to freeze up or loosen.

Elora began to sing again, soothing the spiders as we hurried through. Honestly, I was looking forward to getting to the deadly ghost pirates, as long as there were no spiders.

Finally, we reached the end of the spiders, and Elora slowed.

She looked back over her shoulder. "We're nearly there. Be very quiet."

We crept toward the end of the tunnel where a faint blue light illuminated the space within. The four of us stopped before it and gathered in a circle.

Elora leaned in and whispered, so silently I almost couldn't hear her. "I will leave you here. This is the line that I cannot cross. It's the same line that the pirates cannot go past. If you want to escape with your transport charm, you must do so in this spot. Or farther out in the cave tunnels."

"Where the spiders are," Declan murmured.

Elora nodded.

"Here is good," Declan said.

I nodded. Here was *very* good.

"Now, remember. Don't let them touch you." Elora gave us a serious look. "Be careful."

"Thanks."

She nodded, then turned and left.

I looked at my friends. "Ready to trick some pirates?"

"Born ready," Syra said.

14

S ilently, we crept toward the pirate's cave. The air chilled at the entrance, sending a shiver over my spine.

We pressed ourselves against the rocks, moving silently and slowly. When we reached the entrance to the pirate's lair, we peered around the edge.

It was a large space, full of the strange rock formations that had decorated the tunnel. The ceiling arched high above, at least seventy feet, and holes in the ground allowed light to stream through. Moss dangled down from the holes, almost beautiful.

Against one wall, there was a massive pile of gold and glittering gems.

"Shiver me timbers," Syra muttered.

I nodded, nearly struck dumb. I'd never seen so much sparkle. I kinda wanted it.

Several pirates lounged on it, their ghostly forms mostly transparent. Somehow, they still managed to look dirty. Grungy, even. One had a peg leg, and another had a parrot on his shoulder.

How cliché.

The rest—about twenty of them—were scattered around the space. Two played some kind of game, and at least ten were drinking out of weird bulbous bottles.

Rum, no doubt.

Fortunately, there were enough rock formations in the middle of the cavern to provide cover for Declan and Syra. Some were only a few feet high, others reaching ten or twelve feet. They were all amorphous, formed by changing rock over the years.

I turned back to look at my friends, who nodded at me. I handed Declan my phone, since his didn't have suitable material on it, then flipped up the hood on my suit so my form disappeared.

Declan and Syra nodded at me, then disappeared into the cave.

Go time.

I waited where I was, making sure that I had my magical signature under control. The last thing I needed was for the ghosts to spot me.

Declan and Syra moved on silent feet, heading away from the piles of gold and using the rock formations as cover. I watched them closely, holding my breath.

They were meant to provide a distraction, one that the pirates would never see coming. More importantly, they'd never even see Declan or Syra.

They moved so quietly that the ghosts didn't seem to notice their presence. Probably because nothing new had happened here in hundreds of years. Why would it happen today?

Once I lost sight of Declan and Syra, I returned my attention to the pile of gold, searching for a flash of blue. Damn, I hoped that thing was easy to find.

Every few seconds, I glanced back toward the side of the cave where Declan and Syra were setting up the distractions.

When the lights from the cell phones flared bright, I grinned.

Declan and Syra had found two rock platforms that were about at eye level, and each had set up their cell phone on the ledge. Right where the pirates could see it.

Music blasted from Syra's phone—"All the Single Ladies" by Beyoncé. If I hadn't been so worried, I might have laughed. It was the music video—which made it even better. My phone flashed with light as well, showing a video of a kitten eating yogurt.

Most people who knew me wouldn't expect me to have a treasure trove of kitten videos on my phone, but that was intentional.

The pirates all leapt to their feet, roaring. Shouts and scuffles sounded as they surged toward the lights.

Now was my moment.

I raced from my spot, counting on Declan and Syra to return to the cave entrance and wait for me. The mountain of gold in front of me gleamed, and I searched it, looking for that flash of blue and hoping that I wouldn't have to jostle the pile too much to find it.

From the other side of the cave, confused shouts sounded from the pirates.

"It's a tiny lady!"

"She's not wearing any clothes!" The voice sounded excited.

"Why's she in the little black box?" That pirate sounded a bit dim, actually.

"It's a lovely kitten!"

"Lovely?" Growled a pirate's voice.

"Yes, lovely! Kittens are lovely!"

"What's the white stuff on its face?"

If I hadn't been so intent on finding the gem, and so scared of being killed by a ghost pirate's touch, I would have laughed.

Instead, I was racing around the pile of gold, trying to find the gem without disturbing anything.

There were a few amazing old coins I wanted to snag, but I resisted. Once upon a time, I definitely would have nabbed as much as I could carry. But being friends with Cass, Nix, and Dell —the FireSouls who were a bit like archaeologists even though they said they weren't—had taught me that was a pretty uncool thing to do.

Treasure like this was part of history, and history belonged to everyone. Not just the person who could fit it in their pockets. If I messed with it and took something, I'd be screwing up valuable information about this archaeological site. Sure, it was full of deadly pirates, but the principle remained the same.

Anyway, I didn't have time.

Behind me, the pirates were still exclaiming over the videos. Most of them were *very* interested in Beyoncé, but there were a couple of holdouts for the kitten.

My pulse pounded in my ears as I searched the last section of the pile of gold. There were coins and chains and boxes and brooches. But no glitter of blue.

Shit.

I wasn't going to be able to do this without disturbing it.

I tried the gentle approach first, just shifting some of the gold with my boot. It tumbled down, a waterfall of sparkles, but there was no blue behind it.

The ghosts didn't seem to hear.

Yet.

So I tried again, shifting some more gold.

Nothing.

I kept going, having no luck.

"Oy! The pile's moving!"

The words sent a shiver down my spine.

I glanced back over my shoulder, heart in my throat. A few ghosts were looking at me.

Crap.

They couldn't see me, but they would definitely notice if the gold kept shifting around.

More of them would figure it out soon.

I needed to bring out the big guns.

I called my mace from the ether. The FireSouls would probably frown at what I was about to do. They would definitely say I was *disturbing the context*.

But at least I wasn't stealing anything. And I couldn't hurt gold coins. More importantly, there were lives at risk.

I gripped the chain of the mace and swung, straight for the middle of the pile. The metal ball slammed into it, scattering the gold coins and jewelry everywhere. Nothing was damaged, but yeah, I'd definitely disturbed the context.

As the pirates roared their rage, I searched the shower of glittering gold, my gaze finally snagging on something blue. It flew through the air and landed a few feet away on top of a pile.

I stashed my mace in the ether and lunged for it, scrambling across the gold. The coins shifted beneath my hands and feet, making it difficult to move.

It was *way* harder than Scrooge McDuck had made it look.

I clambered toward the glowing blue stone, knowing without a doubt that *this* was the sea sapphire. It was the exact shade of the ocean.

"Behind!" Declan shouted.

Shit.

He'd revealed his location. Which meant there must be a pirate right on my tail, and I hadn't even noticed. That was the only thing that would make him shout.

I lunged farther, grabbing for the sea sapphire. Somehow, it slipped through my fingers.

Shit.

I spun around, catching sight of the three ghosts that were right behind me.

I froze.

The pirates were just six feet away, their eyes searching the area around me. All three had raggedy beards and even more raggedy clothes. One had a pipe clutched in his jaws.

Though they couldn't see me, they could determine my location by the way the coins moved beneath me.

I was only a few feet from the sea sapphire. My gaze darted to it. If I could just grab it and run...

The other pirates were moving closer. Only a couple had remained to hang out with Beyoncé and the kitten.

A few were looking for Declan, muttering about the sound of a man's voice.

I had no time to delay.

I sprang for the sea sapphire and managed to grab it this time. It felt slippery as water—no wonder it had slipped through my hands before. That must be one of the reasons it had its name.

"There it is!" shouted the pirate. "The coins are moving!"

"It's a ghost!" said another.

They lunged for me.

I gripped the sapphire tight and dived out of the way, skidding on the coins and scrambling to my feet. They pivoted quickly, moving faster than I could.

I made it to my feet, giving a burst of speed, then sprinted toward the entrance of the cave.

Two pirates came at me, no doubt able to see where I was because of the coins that my boots kicked up. They reached out blindly, their arms widespread, trying to catch whatever was making the coins move.

I darted left and right, narrowly avoiding them.

"On your tail!" Declan shouted.

I glanced back.

They were gaining.

Damn, they were fast. They had no bodies to slow them down.

I sprinted faster, my eyes on the cave entrance. Every cell and muscle burned, my lungs heaving. I gripped the stone tightly and hurtled toward the exit.

Declan appeared in front of me, running toward me.

What the hell?

He wasn't supposed to do that.

Then I felt it.

The icy touch of death.

The hand fell upon my shoulder, cold and fierce.

The reason Declan was running.

The ghosts were even faster than they'd seemed.

My legs faltered, and I slowed. Every bit of strength leached from my muscles as the ghost sucked the life from me with his touch.

Oh, shit.

My legs gave out, and I fell, barely managing to keep a grip on the stone. The ghost lost his grip—he still couldn't see me, so the fall had likely taken him by surprise.

A flash of black appeared out of the corner of my eye.

Wally.

The little hellcat's fur smoked, and his eye blazed red with flame. He hissed, then opened his mouth and blew a blast of fire at the ghosts.

They recoiled, and Wally blew another blast.

They wouldn't stay back for long, though. I could feel it.

"Wally, go! It's too dangerous."

Wally completely ignored me, standing between me and the ghosts and blasting his flame.

I turned my head, seeing Declan coming to save me.

He wouldn't go without me.

I knew it like I knew my own name.

It took the last bit of my strength to yank the hood from my head, revealing my form. I tried to crawl to him, but I was too weak.

Declan was nearly to me, and he swooped down and grabbed me up. His wings flared from his back, and he shot into the air, out of reach of the ghosts.

Down below, Wally disappeared.

My vision was blurry and fading fast. I barely managed to whisper, "The stone."

Declan's hand closed around mine, trapping the stone tight. Below, I could see the enraged ghosts shouting and leaping. The parrot was squawking. In the background, Beyoncé sang and the kitten meowed.

I drew in a shuddery breath, feeling like all my organs had shut down. One more second of contact, and that ghost could have killed me.

Hell, it might still kill me.

My vision was growing worse, and breathing was harder.

Declan flew toward the entrance of the cave. He dived low. Through bleary eyes, I caught sight of Syra. She chucked a stone to the ground, and the cloud of gray dust poofed up.

She jumped into it, and Declan followed, flying fast into the ether. It sucked us in, pulling us through space and spitting us out in the cool night air.

I couldn't see anymore. Everything was totally dark. Panic gripped my chest.

"Aerdeca!" Declan's voice sounded frantic.

He laid me on the ground. The grass felt cool and soft beneath my back.

"Is she okay?" Syra demanded.

"No." Declan's voice was sharp with worry. His hands landed on my shoulders, gentle but firm.

I could barely perceive the world around me, but I could sense him.

Healing warmth flowed into me, surging through my body like a tidal wave. At first, I felt nothing but the warmth. I was still weak and blind, with organs that felt like they were shutting down, but at least I was warm.

Then I felt *him*.

A connection.

That same connection I'd felt both other times he'd healed me. Only this time, it was stronger. Fiercer. As if I were feeling his will, flowing into me. He was begging me to live—using his magic to beg me to live.

And his voice.

Suddenly, I could hear it. His real voice.

"Come on, Aerdeca. Come on." Distress tore at every word.

I fought my way toward it. Fought to find my way toward him. Toward Mari and the FireSouls who needed me. Connor.

I had too much left to do.

I couldn't die.

My friends needed me.

Declan's healing magic gave me strength, but I had to fight my way back to life. I imagined everything I needed to do, everyone I needed to help.

I gasped raggedly, strength returning to my muscles. Declan's power flowed into me, mending my body back together.

Soon, I could see. I could breathe. And move.

More than that, I could feel him. The connection formed by his healing power was strong. He cared for me.

I could *feel* it.

So strange.

I coughed, pushing Declan's hands away. "That's enough."

"You're not one hundred percent yet." Concern radiated in his voice.

"Save your power." I could feel how much he was pouring into me. He needed to save enough for himself, or he wouldn't be able to fight.

Even now, he looked ashen. But relieved.

He was bent over me, his shoulders curved. I lunged up, hugging him and burying my face in his neck.

"Thank you for saving me," I whispered.

"Only you were brave enough to run into that cave full of deadly ghosts."

I smiled, but knew he'd have done it, too. I gave him one last squeeze, drawing in deeply of his scent, and then pulled back.

"Take the Power-Up Potion that Hedy gave you." I dug into my pockets and pulled out two vials. One was a little vial of healing potion that I liked to carry around—I'd need the extra boost, since my insides still felt pulverized—and the other was the Power-Up.

I swigged both back, feeling strength flow into my limbs.

"Thank fates, that feels better." I flopped back on the grass.

Syra slumped down next to me, gasping. "I was freaking worried there."

"Me too."

She laughed. "I can only imagine." She rubbed her hands over her face and laughed some more. "Those ghosts! I couldn't believe it."

"I know. They loved those phones." I smiled at the thought. They were bastards, but they'd been hilarious.

"They'll be disappointed when the batteries die," Declan said.

"Serves them right for being jerks," I said. "Well done, guys."

"Any time." Syra looked at me. "I need to hang out with you guys more often. You know how to have a good time."

"Well, I'm pleased to tell you that the fun is just beginning. Because we've got a demon to catch."

"Wouldn't miss it for the world," Syra said.

"Excellent." I propped myself upright as I met Declan's eyes. "What time is it?"

He checked his phone, then looked up at me. "Just after midnight."

"That gives us just over two hours." I sagged back onto the grass. Just two measly hours until the final showdown.

A showdown where we'd live or die.

I pressed my fingertips to my comms charm, igniting the magic. "Mari? You there?"

"Yeah. You find the sapphire?"

"I did. Meet at the beach?"

"Be there in five."

Declan climbed to his feet, then held out a hand to help me up. I took it and let him yank me to my feet. He did the same for Syra.

"Let's check out the beach," I said. "I think I see light."

We strode toward the sandy spot where the Protectorate members had been sitting earlier. Sure enough, there was Hans, the Protectorate cook. He bustled around the fire, making tea and coffee. There was a table set up with a kettle of something that smelled divine.

Hans was a tall man, with a handlebar mustache and a chef's hat.

"Hans." I greeted him with a nod, and he fed us while we waited. The Protectorate really knew how to run a smooth operation.

We were still eating when Mari showed up with the rest of the crew. She strode toward me, looking even more tired than she had earlier.

Everyone gathered around the food table, restocking as fast

as they could. We'd be back in Magic's Bend in minutes, setting up for the final fight.

Mari collapsed on the log next to me, leaning her head on my shoulder. "Thank fates you found it."

"Seriously." I leaned my head on hers. We'd done this a lot over the years, but never in quite such a serious scenario.

We could steal only a few seconds to rest, and I was going to take advantage of every one of them.

After a moment, I drew in a shuddery breath and lifted my head, meeting Mari's gaze. "Nullifier?"

She just shook her head.

Shit.

I looked at Declan, even though I knew the answer. He shook his head, too.

If the Protectorate couldn't find one, and the High Court of the Angels couldn't find one...

There was no nullifier to be found.

I swallowed hard. "Then we're going to have to beat the hell out of this demon. We have DragonGods and an army of some of the most skilled supernaturals out there."

And we had me.

Because if we couldn't break down the Oraxia demon's defenses, I was going to bring out the big guns.

Mari was glaring at me, and it was pretty obvious what she was thinking. She wouldn't say it out loud, though. Since we were in a hurry to get to the battle site, I might not ever have to listen to her concerns at all.

"I'll rally the troops," Mari said. "We think the demon will deliver the orb to the middle of the neighborhood, so that its magic can reach out to the far edges, but we don't know where he'll enter. So we'll set up a perimeter of guards. As soon as someone spots him, we'll go for it."

I nodded, thinking. "Declan and Bree can watch from up high. That will help. They can give a signal."

Declan nodded.

I'd probably find a place on a roof, out of sight but with a good vantage point.

Declan handed me the sea sapphire that he'd taken from my limp hand.

"Thanks." I closed my palm around it, then stuck it in my pocket. I patted the other pocket to make sure that the little stone jar of potion was tucked safely inside.

I swallowed hard. This was it. There wasn't that much planning left to do.

I met everyone's gazes. All were shadowed with worry. I was sure mine was the same.

We had one shot left.

15

I crouched on the rooftop in the Historic District, the wind blowing my hair back from my face. The moon kept disappearing behind the clouds, but the street lamps below kept the visibility good.

The road was deathly quiet, the old houses and shops all blacked out. No one was home, so no lights were shining. The old facades of the colorful Victorian buildings looked derelict and lonely tonight.

"Nice choice of spots," Mari said.

"Thanks." I'd picked it because it had a view of the biggest road through the Historic District. We had the best view of the whole place.

All around, Protectorate members were stationed in the shadows, watching for the demon to arrive. In the sky, Bree, Ana, and Declan flew high, keeping an eye on the ground below.

Bree's silver Valkyrie wings glinted in the moonlight, while Ana blended perfectly with the dark. She was the Morrigan, a giant black battle crow and queen from Celtic myth. Their sister, Rowan, was still on a deadly mission for the Protectorate, though I wished she could have been here. She was seriously powerful, and we could use all the strength we could get.

On the ground, their men—fiancés, boyfriends, I wasn't sure what they were—prowled with the rest of the Protectorate members. Cade and Lachlan were in their animal forms. Cade, Bree's man, had shifted into an enormous wolf. Lachlan, who belonged with Ana, was a black lion. Near them, Claire fought. She threw fireballs with one hand and wielded a sword with the other. She fought for her brother, and it was obvious.

My gaze flicked over to Declan. His powerful wings moved gracefully as he kept an eye on the northern part of town.

Tension crackled on the air as we waited. We were only minutes away from the six-hour mark.

Would the demon be on time?

I glanced at Mari.

Her eyes met mine. "There has to be another way. You don't need to do this. It's the worst kind of magic."

"Maybe I won't even have to." My stomach pitched, though, as if it knew I'd be creating nullification magic later tonight. I looked back at the city, scanning the streets and the skies.

Ana, who was closest to us, gave a sharp crow's caw, the sound ringing through the night.

Declan and Bree flew closer to her, and I stiffened. "He may be near."

Mari tilted her head upward and sniffed. Her nose wrinkled. "Yes, I think I smell him."

I also got a hint of rotten garbage and sulfur, two scents I hadn't smelled before.

Declan joined Ana, then hurled a blast of heavenly fire at the ground, into a street that I couldn't see.

It was the signal.

Not only would the fire hopefully hurt the demon, it would light up the night sky so everyone else knew where he was.

We were too far away.

"Let's go." Mari climbed to her feet. "I think we can take the roofs."

Some of them were flat and some peaked, but we managed to race across them, leaping from building to building as the sound of battle rent the sky. The houses here were so close that it wasn't hard to jump from one to another.

Finally, we reached the site of the battle. In the small side street, I spotted the Oraxia demon immediately. Declan hurtled bright white blasts of heavenly fire at him, his aim perfect.

It was working!

The demon was being driven to his knees from the force of it. A bag hung at his side, roughly the size of the orb I'd seen in Factory Row.

All around, demons swarmed. At least forty of them.

The Oraxia demon had brought backup. Probably worried about this exact scenario. He'd lost the element of surprise long ago and needed guards while he did his dirty work.

Ana dived, her black crow form massive and graceful. She flew straight for the demons who surrounded the Oraxia, her huge, sharp claws ready to strike. Protectorate members spilled out of the side streets, headed straight for the demons. They threw fire and ice at the demons, who rallied around their magic. Sonic booms exploded, and potion bombs filled the air. Cade and Lachlan charged in their animal forms, each tearing apart a demon. Even Wally was there, breathing fire on a skinny demon with tall horns and black fangs.

The battle was fierce, cries coming from all around. Steel clashed with steel, and blood began to flow.

I looked back toward the Oraxia demon, who was struggling to his feet. Declan's fire was slowing him down, but it wasn't penetrating the protective barrier he possessed.

Shit.

Bree flew toward Declan, adding blasts of deadly lightning to the mix. The demon went to his knees again, slower to rise. Ana dived low, picking off demons with her sharp black beak.

"Let's help them." I met Mari's gaze. "Lightning?"

"Definitely."

I'd promised her that we'd try to defeat the demon before I created nullifying magic, and honestly, I'd been happy to do so. I didn't want to take on that horrible power unless I had to.

"I'll go to the other side." If we were going to use our cooperative lightning—which was stronger than any single blast—I needed to be opposite her, with the demon between us.

She nodded. "Safe hunting."

"Safe hunting." I scrambled down the edge of the building, joining the fray in the street below.

I passed by Jude, the powerful leader of the Protectorate. She fought a demon with her electric whip, moving gracefully around him, the weapon cracking as it struck. He was easily two feet taller than her, with broad shoulders and hulking muscles, but she was faster, her dark braids swirling in the air as her starry blue eyes sparkled.

I had no doubt she'd win this one.

As I sprinted across the street, I caught sight of Caro, a platinum-haired Protectorate member, shooting a jet of water straight through the chest of a small yellow demon who spat green acid. The water left the other side of him, tinged pink with blood.

"Hurry up and die, you bastard!" Caro shouted.

I sprinted past her, dodging around another fighting pair. Ahead of me, a skinny demon with dark gray skin grinned at me, revealing long fangs. He raised a hand, then hurled a blast of smoke at me.

I dived left, rolling on the ground and popping to my feet.

Freaking shadow demon. It'd been ages since I'd seen one of them.

"I've got important shit to be doing, man, and you're in my way." I called on my mace, taking it from the ether.

He shot another blast of smoke at me, this one bigger than the last. I dodged left, narrowly avoiding it. It blew past my shoulder, still managing to land a fiery blow that made my arm ache.

I swung my mace at him, going for speed, and slammed the spiked ball into his head. He flew to the side, his skull crushed. I didn't even bother letting my mace finish its swing. I just sent it right back to the ether and raced for the building across the street.

I found a spot at the base of it, right across from Mari with the demon between us. The bastard was back to his feet, staggering forward, the force of Declan's fire and Bree's lightning slowing him down but not stopping him.

He wasn't far from the middle of the neighborhood, and we had to stop him.

I caught Mari's eye and raised my hand, the gesture for our lightning. She nodded, then drew a dagger from the ether. I did the same and sliced across my left palm—the one I didn't use for my mace.

Pain welled and blood flowed, and I imagined lightning. The crackle and power of it. Lightning filled me from within, sharp and bright, then shot from my palm, joining with Mari's electricity. Thunder cracked in the air.

The demon was caught right in the middle. The electricity lit him up, and he went to his knees again. Victory surged through me, but it was short-lived. Soon, he was on his feet, staggering forward.

It was like he was getting stronger!

Damn it.

I met Mari's gaze. Even from here, I could see that she looked stricken.

She knew what this meant, just as I did.

Our side had already taken out half the demons, and multiple mages were throwing fireballs and sonic booms at our main target. They were bouncing right off the Oraxia demon's shield.

I had to try. With any luck, I could swipe his forehead with blood and use my power of suggestion on him.

It was a long shot, but worth it.

The demon was right in front of me, striding down the street.

I raced for the demon, approaching from the side and waving my arms at the fliers in the sky. I did *not* need them to hit me with a lightning bolt or heavenly fire by mistake.

I pressed my comms charm, knowing that it would connect to Declan. We'd gotten him one just for the battle. "Declan, hold your fire. Get everyone to hold their fire."

"On it." He shouted loud enough to get everyone's attention, then shot a lightning bolt directly into the sky. Everyone ceased their offensive when they spotted the signal we'd agreed upon.

I pressed the charm again. "I'll be going invisible." I would need that advantage against the enormous demon if I had to get close enough to touch him. "Don't let anyone fire again until I tell you to."

With the onslaught stopped, the Oraxia demon could move faster. He hurried down the road, his bag jostling against his side.

I flipped up my hood so I was invisible, and sprinted after him. I was revealing the fact that my ghost suit could turn me invisible, but there was no other way to win this.

The demon never saw me coming, and I looped around to approach him from the front. Quickly, I pierced my finger with my sharp thumbnail, letting blood well. No one could see what I was doing, so they wouldn't know that I was using my power of suggestion.

When I reached him, I leapt, raising my hand.

I slammed into the shield that protected him. The invisible forcefield threw me back, and he barely even flinched.

I crashed onto the ground, pain flaring.

He strode by me, never even noticing my invisible form.

Aching, I raised my hand to my comms charm. "Resume the attack."

Declan asked no questions, just began to fire again. It slowed the demon, but didn't stop him.

None of us were succeeding. Not even the DragonGods. They had the power of freaking *gods*, and they still couldn't do it.

The demon's protective power was just too strong. We had to break through it. Break the magic itself.

Our army resumed its attack, but it only slowed the demon. Soon, he'd be to the middle of the neighborhood, in the perfect position to deploy the orb.

And we'd all turn to stone.

There was only one thing left to do.

I slipped back into a darkened alley, dread filling my soul. My breathing caught as I knelt on the dirty stone ground. Cold sweat dripped down my back.

I hadn't tried to create magic this big since I'd been a teenager in captivity.

Please work.

The sound of the battle kept me company, though it was horrible background music. Quickly, I sliced my sharp thumb-nail across both of my arms.

Agony shot through me and blood welled, pouring white onto the ground.

Mari stumbled into the alley a half second later, her eyes wide. "No, Aeri! Let me."

I looked up to meet her gaze. "Too late. It was always you protecting me when we were kids. Now it's my turn."

She fell to her knees in front of me. "Don't go too far. Just make some of the magic. Not all of it."

I nodded, my hands shaking, and began to pour my magic out of me along with my blood. Flashbacks of doing this as a child popped into my mind, but I shoved them away. Then, I'd been forced to do this.

Now, I chose it.

I had power over this. It would make all the difference.

My head grew woozy as the blood and magic poured onto the stones. I envisioned a nullifier's power, imagining destroying any magic I came into contact with. I imagined banishing it from existence with just a touch. I envisioned empty rooms and barren fields, sparkling magic disappearing in the blink of an eye.

All because I willed it so.

"That's enough," Mari said. "Stop now."

"Not done." My voice was ragged and my head was spinning. I needed to almost die for this to work. To give it all of my magic and all of my power.

I'd said I could do this in half measures—creating just a little bit of the nullifier's magic—but now that the ritual had begun, it was clear that wasn't true.

If I didn't do it right, I could die. My memories of the past made that clear enough.

Almost there.

I kept going, determined to finish.

Mari threw a splash of liquid onto my arms, sealing the cuts. Shocked, I looked up at her. But she was already looking down at the pool of my white blood, holding out her hands and feeding some of her magic into the spell.

"What are you doing?" I was so weak I could barely speak the words.

She said nothing, but it was obvious.

She was helping me. Giving me some of her magic—giving the spell some of her magic—so that I wouldn't have to. She did it to save me from the negative effects of the nullifier's magic, though I had no idea if this would work. She couldn't know, either.

We'd never created magic this way before. Last time, when we'd done it as children to create the lightning, she'd been bleeding, too.

This time, she wasn't.

Love swelled in my chest, along with worry. I batted her hands away, gasping. "Stop."

Nearly all of my strength was gone, but at that moment, the magic in the air changed. It sparked with energy, fierce and strong, then began to flow back into me. It surged into my body.

I straightened and inhaled as the magic flooded my body, my soul. New blood formed in my veins, new strength in my muscles. New magic in my soul.

The nullifying power made my stomach turn, but it was bearable.

Soon, I was strong again. Whole again.

Mari grabbed my hand. "Are you okay?"

"Yes." I looked up, catching sight of Declan flying above, his gaze pinned to me.

My stomach pitched.

How much had he seen?

I swallowed hard, shoving the thought away. I'd deal with that later. Right now, I had to take care of this damned demon.

I had new strength, renewed power.

New power.

"Thank you, Mari." I met her gaze.

She hugged me tightly, then stood, dragging me to my feet. I surged upward, ready to kill this damned demon.

"Test it," Mari demanded. "Test your new magic."

I wanted to say I didn't have time. I needed to charge out and fight that bastard.

But she was right. I had to know the extents of my new power. It would help me win the battle.

"Can you feel it?" I asked, trying to push the nullifying magic out toward her. I imagined suffocating Mari's magic—just temporarily—so she could feel it.

From what I'd learned of nullifiers, they could do this from a distance.

She shook her head, dread filling her eyes.

Shit. "It didn't work?"

"Touch me and do it."

I grabbed her arm and repeated the process, pushing my nullifying magic into her. She sucked in a ragged breath and turned green. I yanked my arm back.

Her color returned quickly. "That felt like hell."

"Like your soul leaving your body?" Magic and souls were often so closely linked that if you lost your magic, you felt like you'd lost your soul. Like an empty husk. A broken doll.

Mari nodded. "It works when you touch."

Thank fates. "Then I'll have to touch the demon."

It seemed that Mari's help had changed the usual nullifier's magic. Weakened it, as we'd hoped.

I looked back up. Declan had disappeared. What did he think?

I shook my head. Didn't matter now.

"Let's go." I sprinted to the end of the alley and peered out into the street.

The Oraxia demon was farther down the road, still staggering toward his destination. More of his henchmen were down, but not all of them.

I flipped up my hood so I was invisible, and sprinted after him.

When I was nearly to the demon, I pressed my fingertips to my comms charm. "Declan, stop the attack."

Declan roared, then shot his lightning toward the sky. The attack stopped.

My footsteps weren't silent on the ground—I was in too much of a hurry for silence, and the Oraxia demon turned when I neared him, no doubt able to hear me.

But he couldn't see me.

Right before I reached him, I drew my dagger from the ether and leapt toward him. As I soared through the air, I imagined my nullifying power roaring to life. I hit him hard, clinging like a monkey, and shoved my new nullifying magic into him, praying that it would kill his defensive power.

There was a bolt of painful energy that almost melted my insides as his protective magic got me, but then the nullifying magic kicked in. The pain faded, and he stilled, clearly shocked that I was hanging on to him. And probably shocked that he couldn't see me.

He didn't know *what* I was.

Before his shock wore off, I sliced at his ear, grabbing off a piece.

He bellowed and smacked me. Pain flared in my side as I flew to the left and crashed on the ground. I scrambled away, clutching the piece of his ear. He searched the area around him, clearly confused.

I'd never expected my most cherished possession to be a piece of demon ear, but you never could know what to expect from life.

I pressed my fingers to my comms charm. "Attack him."

I rolled over, hoping to see Bree's lightning take him out. Maybe my nullifying magic had a lingering effect. Thunder cracked as her lightning shot into the demon. He went to his feet with a grunt, but didn't fall.

My nullifying power did *not* seem to have any kind of lasting effect.

But there was no time to be disappointed.

Declan hurled blast after blast of heavenly fire at him, a deadly onslaught that kept the demon pinned to the ground while I worked.

Still invisible, I dug the sea sapphire and the tiny stone jar of potion out of my pocket.

It was the moment when we found out if the Devyver had screwed us.

16

A s the battle raged and my friends kept the Oraxia demon pinned down with their magic, I sucked in a deep breath to still my shaking hands. Carefully, I pried the top off the little stone jar. First, I shoved the glittering blue rock in. Then the piece of the demon's ear.

Ew.

I closed the jar back up and shook it, praying to the fates that this would work. My side ached from where the demon had hit me, and my arm burned from the smoke of the demon's blast, but all my attention was on the little stone jar.

Magic began to sparkle around it. I looked up, spotting the Oraxia demon about twenty feet away. The others were slowing him down, but he could still move, though slowly.

With a jolt of horror, I realized that he was almost there.

The magic around the stone bottle faded. It was done.

Pleas work, please work, please work.

I surged to my feet and raced after the demon, careful not to get between him and any of the attacking mages from my side. I was still invisible and didn't want to screw this all up because I was a moron. Over the sound of thunder and the blasts of magic, he couldn't hear my footsteps.

When I was nearly to the demon, I pressed my fingertips to my comms charm. "Declan, stop the attack."

Declan roared, then shot his lightning toward the sky. The attack stopped.

The demon stiffened, as if he knew something was up. But I was so close that he didn't have a chance to react. I slammed into his back so hard that he flew to the ground. I followed him down, straddling him from behind.

I shoved my nullifying magic into him, and his protective charm didn't zap me. Before he could move, I yanked the top off the stone jar and dumped the potion on the back of his neck, making sure to hit his orange skin.

His flesh sizzled, and he bellowed.

"I'm your new master now!" I shouted. "You will obey me."

He shouted and thrashed, trying to break free. I punched him in the head, carefully avoiding his four horns, but he bucked, throwing me off him. I crashed onto the ground, pain flaring in my shoulder.

The demon surged to his feet, spinning to find me.

I leapt up, charging him.

He still couldn't see me, so I had the advantage. Right before I reached him, I drew my dagger from the ether. I stabbed it into his shoulder, far from anywhere there might be a heart, and threw my entire body weight onto him.

I took him to the ground again, but he was fast. His big hand smashed into my upper arm. I felt—and *heard*—my arm break. My stomach lugged, and I nearly puked on his orange face.

Fortunately, it was the arm that didn't hold the knife, so I twisted the blade. I straddled him, refusing to let go. The bag containing the orb was squished against my leg, but didn't feel breakable. The contents felt sturdy as a rock.

"You bastard," I hissed, thinking of the frozen bodies of my friends.

My nullifying magic was working—it let me get past his defenses and hurt him—but it also meant I was close enough for him to hurt me.

He pounded his fist into my thigh, and stars sparked in my vision. I didn't hear the bone snap, but damn, it hurt. I wouldn't be walking well for a week. The demon couldn't see what he was hitting, but damned if he didn't have good aim.

I fought the nausea and called upon my power to compel him. I could feel it, a connection created by the potion. The Devyver said that the demon would be fighting his allegiance to me and to the ones who had originally hired him.

Well, I was here now, and I was going to win.

"You're mine to command." My icy voice rang with power.

He growled.

I twisted the knife again.

He thrashed, trying to throw me off him. I could feel him succumbing to the potion, to my mastery, but it hadn't taken full effect yet.

Maybe he needed to see my face.

I tried to raise my broken arm to shove my hood back, but I could barely twitch the useless thing. And no way in hell I'd remove the dagger from his shoulder.

I threw my head back so violently that it nearly gave me a headache, but the hood fell back off my face.

Suddenly, I became aware of the crowd around me. The last of the Oraxia demon's minions had been killed off, and all eyes were on me. The Protectorate members had crept closer, and now they could see who was making the demon thrash around wildly.

Damn, this was going to be hard to explain. Especially to Declan. I wanted to see him, but didn't dare look.

"I'm Aerdeca, and I am your master." I imbued the words with as much force as I could. "You will recite the spell to remove the curse you've placed upon my town. You *will*."

All the while, I made sure to keep up with the nullifying magic. If his defenses returned, I'd be screwed. We'd *all* be screwed.

The demon shook his head, fighting me. I pushed my magic toward him, envisioning it as a glittering cloud. I could still feel the connection formed by the potion, and I took advantage of it, strengthening it with my power. It made my stomach turn, but it was working. The demon was calming.

Suddenly, there was a snap in the air. Like a rubber band breaking and hitting me in the forehead.

I jerked. The demon did as well.

The potion had taken effect. My power had overridden his previous master's.

He was mine to command.

And it felt like hell.

The demon sagged. He glared at me with hate, but was able to grind out the word, "Fine."

I nodded, feeling the connection even more strongly.

It made my insides lurch. Even worse than the nullifier's magic, which wasn't as bad as I'd expected it to be.

I stood, my leg feeling like it had been stepped on by a horse, and gestured for the demon to rise. "Stand there. Do *nothing*."

The demon stood still as a board.

Faintly, I could feel him fighting my pull. I'd have to keep an eye on that.

I pressed my fingertips to my comms charm. "Mari? Bree? Are the scouts ready?"

"They're ready." Their voices echoed in my ears at the same time.

We had scouts in each of the other neighborhoods, standing

next to the frozen bodies of our friends and neighbors. I needed confirmation that all was back to normal before I killed the demon.

"Do it." I shot the demon a hard look, pushing my magic toward him, making sure that he could feel the power of my command. "Cast the spell that will undo the magic that turned our citizens to stone. I can feel when you obey me and when you fight. So do it correctly."

The demon bared his teeth, then knelt, reaching into the bag at his side and withdrawing the orb. He set it down in front of him, then bent over, pressing his hands to the ground. Magic surged from him, dark and fierce. It turned the ground around his hands black. I stumbled a few steps away, my stomach churning, but didn't feel him fighting the connection between us.

He began to chant in a language I didn't understand, but it felt right, somehow. I hated how so much of this was based on faith and feelings, but it really did feel like it was working. Because I was connected to him.

It was freaking awful.

The demon roared the chant louder, and magic sizzled over my skin. The blackened ground around his hands began to glow. The orb began to glow.

Fear chilled my skin.

It looked like he was about to cast the final spell that would turn us all to stone. But it didn't feel like that.

My friends couldn't feel it though. They didn't have the same connection that I did.

I looked up and around, making sure no one would attack. Bree looked like she was about to hurl a bolt of lightning, but I raised my hands, a silent plea.

She stopped immediately, lowering her hand.

I looked back at the demon, who was chanting louder than

ever. The hair on the back of my neck stood up. When the magic in the air was so staticky that it was almost unbearable, the demon sat up.

He reached for the orb, then smashed it on the ground.

Power surged out from the shattered object, so strong that it blew me off my feet. I crashed onto my side, my broken arm hurting so bad that I nearly blacked out.

The demon was on his back, too, but soon, he'd be up.

I struggled to get to my feet, but the pain was almost too much.

Gentle hands gripped my waist and helped me stand. I looked back.

Declan. He looked pale.

"Thanks." My stomach flipped at the memory of him seeing me creating new magic.

No time for that.

I turned to the demon, who was rising to his feet, and charged him. I slammed him back down to the ground with my weight. No way in hell I was letting him get away. I straddled him, holding him firmly to the ground.

Voices began to come out of my comms charm.

"Museum District is awake. They're statues no longer," Bree said.

"Business District is back," Mari said. "Hang on. So is Dark-lane, they're saying."

Home.

"We've got word from Government Lane. The mayor is confused." Bree's voice was pretty much giddy.

My heart froze in my chest as I waited to hear about Factory Row. That was the most important one.

"Factory Row!" Mari cried.

Tears pricked my eyes, but I blinked them back so the demon couldn't see.

I shot him my coldest look. "Tell me who made you do this."

"I don't know."

"Tell me." The chill in my voice made him pale. "What do you know about them?"

I *had* to know. Because this demon wasn't the real threat. Whoever had put him up to this was the true danger.

"They're from Grimrealm. A group."

Ice shot down my spine. "What are they called?"

"I don't know."

This was no coincidence. The necromancer from last week had been hired by a group from Grimrealm. Now this guy? Not a coincidence.

I drew my dagger from the ether and held it at his neck. My eye caught on a glint of metal chain behind his shirt. I dug it out, finding a medallion at the end.

Just like the one the necromancer demon had worn. I yanked it up and held it in front of his face. "What is this?"

He shrugged. "Just a charm that guarantees I do the job I signed up to do."

"You don't know anything else about it?"

"No."

Shit. "Do you know if this group has a symbol or anything else that is important to them?"

The icon on the medallion was linked to The Weeds, a weaselly guy in Grimrealm who was basically a demon pimp. He wasn't the one running the attacks on Magic's Bend, but he was helping whoever was doing it. Like this demon, he'd said he didn't know who hired him, and I'd believed him. So what I needed was a clue about the people themselves.

I poked the dagger deeper into the demon's neck. "Well, what about that symbol? Do they have one?"

"Not that they showed me."

They wouldn't, no. They'd want to stay quiet.

"How many are there?"

"More than six." His eyes flashed with irritation. "That's all I know."

I believed him. He'd told me all he could. The connection between us made it easy to feel the truth in his words.

It was a connection that made my stomach turn and my skin chill. As long as this demon was alive, I'd feel his presence. I'd feel him as part of me.

I'd wanted to save him for Declan, so he could take him to the High Court of the Angels. But I couldn't bear to live like this, with part of me attached to a demon.

I stabbed my dagger into his throat, dodging the blood that sprayed. Then I twisted it, making sure he was good and dead.

As he choked to death, I stood and surveyed the scene.

Everyone was staring at me, silent.

I'd taken down the demon they couldn't even touch.

Shit.

Like that wasn't suspicious.

I searched for Mari, but saw her nowhere.

Declan approached, concern on his face. "Are you all right?"

"Fine."

"Let me heal—"

Before he could finish the words, Mari appeared right next to me, Connor and Cass in tow. She'd transported them here. She grinned widely. "The others are coming."

My heart leapt at the sight of Cass and Connor. His floppy black hair looked exactly the same as usual, and his shirt said Packaway Handle. It had to be a band, but not one I'd ever heard of.

Claire hurtled toward us from the side, throwing her arms around her brother. "Thank fates, you're safe!"

He hugged her. "Sis!"

Cass's eyes met mine. "Thank you. Mordaca gave me a quick rundown, and thank you."

I nodded, then winced at the pain the small movement caused.

Connor shoved something at me. A little vial of blue liquid. "Mordaca said you'd need this."

Warmth swelled in my chest. "Healing potion?"

"The best." He grinned.

It would be. Connor was one of the best potion masters I'd met. My gaze met Declan's as I swigged back the potion. He'd been about to heal me, but this was better.

After what he'd seen me do, I didn't know if he even really wanted to touch me.

Immediately, the pain in my limbs faded.

"Oh, thank fates." Every muscle in my body relaxed.

"Did you learn who sent him?" Declan asked.

"Only that it was a group from Grimrealm."

"Shit." Declan rubbed a hand over his face.

Mari's eyes darkened. "Like the last time. With the necromancer."

"Exactly," I said. "And he wore the same medallion, so he was probably sent by the same group."

Bree and Ana approached, along with everyone else. I spotted Nix and Del, the other FireSouls, back to life and standing at the edge of the crowd. They smiled and waved.

Bree and Ana stopped in front of us.

"You were like a ghost," Ana said, awe in her voice. "We didn't even see you, but you were kicking his ass, appearing here and there. Like a freaking superhero!"

Pride and worry competed within me. I didn't hate being called a superhero. But *how* I'd done that would be the next question.

And it was.

"How'd you do that?" Bree asked.

"Blood magic." The answer was evasive, but she just nodded.

I had my secrets, and she had hers. With any luck, people wouldn't ask. I was a blood sorceress, so who were they to say that I didn't have a little trick up my sleeve. As long as they didn't know I had dragon blood, there was no reason to worry.

"Thank you again for coming to help." My gaze moved from Bree to Ana and then to Jude. "We can't tell you how much we appreciate it. This wouldn't have been possible without you."

They nodded. The FireSouls thanked them, and everyone split off into small groups. Everyone was exhausted, and it was clear that most just wanted to head home and tend to their wounds. We hadn't lost anyone, at least, and that was a victory to be thankful for.

Mari joined me, wrapping her arm around my waist.

She looked at Declan. "Can you give us a minute?"

He gave her a long look, then gave me an even longer one. Finally, he nodded and walked way.

I sagged against Mari. "He saw."

"Saw what?"

"The ritual."

She stiffened. "Shit."

"I know." My mind raced. "I'll have to find a way to convince him it was something else. Hell, he probably didn't even recognize what it was. Who would?"

"I don't know." Mari sounded doubtful. "There was blood, and suddenly you had new magic."

"As long as he doesn't see me use this magic again—as long as he doesn't know it may be permanent—he might not realize what it means."

"Maybe."

"How do you feel?" she asked.

"Kind of shitty. But not awful." I stiffened. "Wait, can you feel my nullifying magic?"

"A little."

I tried to pull back, not wanting her to feel sick.

"I can deal with it," she said.

I managed to pull away. I caught sight of Cass. She was watching me, an interested gleam in her green eyes.

I waved her over.

She approached. "There's something different about you. Your magical signature is different. Darker. Stronger."

I nodded, making sure no one was around to hear but Cass and Mari. "I managed to get some nullification magic."

Her eyes widened. "How?"

"I'm not a FireSoul, if that's what you're asking."

"I know that." Her eyes searched mine, and she shook her head. "It's all right. You don't have to tell me."

I almost did. I knew I could. I could trust Cass. She wasn't Dani. She'd been in exactly my position before, and I knew she wouldn't turn me in.

All the same, I kept it to myself. I knew it was maybe stupid, but fear wasn't rational. We'd learned the hard way about being loose-lipped. "I need to know if I have the same horrible effects that you did when you took the nullifier's power."

"Do you feel like you want to die? Like your soul has left your body and you're a hollow husk?"

"No."

She shrugged. "Then I'd say you're all right. You have nullifying magic, and there will be side effects, but you're not a nullifier. Not wholly."

My shoulders sagged with relief. I could still feel my magic inside me—the magic I'd been born with--so that was a good sign. "Thanks."

"Anytime." She turned to go, then hesitated. "I'm always here for you, you know. I can keep a secret."

Though we'd known each other for years, we'd always had a fairly formal relationship—that's the relationship I had with everyone who wasn't Mari. An Aerdeca relationship. But to hear her say that meant a lot.

So I just smiled. "Thank you."

We nodded our goodbyes—we'd never been huggers—and she left.

I turned to Mari. "It worked. I didn't have to face the consequences. Not most of them, at least."

"But you were willing to."

I nodded. Yeah. I'd been willing to.

I looked around, searching for Declan, but he was nowhere to be seen.

He'd left.

Shit.

EPILOGUE

The next evening, Mari and I sat at a little table at Potions & Pastilles. We were each dressed in our usual city attire, and I had to be honest, wearing the soft white silk was a nice change from the wet and dirty fight wear I'd been wearing for nearly two days straight. Mari looked fabulous, as always, in her plunging black dress and intense black makeup.

"I'm glad we came." Mari sipped her Manhattan. Potions & Pastilles turned from coffee shop to bar at night, and Connor mixed a great drink.

"Same." I sipped my martini, the clear liquid having a sharp bite. Exhaustion still pulled at me, but we'd both wanted to see our friends a bit since we'd all departed almost immediately after the battle.

I rubbed the silk of my shirt between my fingers, staring hard at it as I thought. Finally, I looked up at Mari. "Do you ever think we're a bit too serious about our disguises? That we hide our true selves from our friends?"

Her dark eyes flashed to mine, the makeup around them perfectly applied. "What? No. Why would we tell?"

Mari's face shifted slightly, taking on a haunted expression, as if she were remembering our time with our family. Then our time with the Order when they'd captured us and tried to use us for our power.

I shook my head. "No, you're right. Don't listen to me."

She patted her ebony bouffant, clearly trying to settle herself. I sipped my drink, and a few minutes passed as I watched Connor and Claire bustle around behind the counter. The FireSouls should arrive soon.

Mari's keen gaze met mine. "This is about Declan, isn't it?"

I hadn't seen him since last night, when he'd disappeared after the battle. Hadn't heard from him either. "He might have figured us out. Given what he saw in the alley... It's possible."

She swallowed hard, nodding. "I know."

"This is crazy, but I think we might be able to trust him."

"We might not have a choice, if he's figured it out," Mari said. "You like him, don't you?"

"I do. So maybe it's wishful thinking, the idea that we can trust him." But I'd *felt* it when he'd healed me.

"Either way, it's time to stop being afraid. We've hidden from our family for years, but we're badass bitches now. We can take them if we have to." Her face hardened. "And if anyone comes for us to use us for our magic, we'll take them too."

Her voice trembled slightly, even though I thought she believed the words she was saying. I believed them, too. But still, it was easy to be afraid of the bogeyman from the past. We just needed to get over it.

I didn't know what was going to happen with Declan, but I'd face it when the time came.

A few minutes later, our friends joined us. Mari and I didn't say anything about our true natures—not yet—but I could feel that the time was probably coming. We'd never spent much social time with the FireSouls, but we should start. Having friends was nice.

After an hour, we headed home. Mari pulled her car into the side street, then we strode to the stairs leading up to our door.

When I spotted Declan sitting on the stoop, I stopped dead in my tracks. Mari grabbed my hand subtly and pulled me along.

"Hey," she said.

I just stared at him, wondering what he was thinking.

"Hi, Mordaca," he said.

She looked at me. "See you inside."

I nodded. She climbed the stairs and entered the house, and I sat next to Declan, careful not to let my shoulder touch his. I didn't know where we stood.

He turned to look at me. "You look beautiful."

I looked down at the sleek silk pants and top. "Thanks."

"But then, you always do."

I smiled. "Trying to butter me up?"

"Just telling the truth."

The weight of yesterday pressed upon me. I glanced at him, but there was nothing to be read in his expression. His dark eyes met mine.

"So, about yesterday..." I let the words trail off.

"You're a Dragon Blood."

Fear shivered over my skin—he *knew*—followed by a strange kind of relief. I hadn't had to tell him. And there was no hiding it. Not with what he'd seen. "You figured it out."

He nodded. "Yes. And I won't tell anyone."

Thank fates.

"After last night, it confirmed for me there is definitely something different about you. It's not just my imagination. The magic that you kept creating was unusual. But the vision of you with your veins cut open, bleeding white blood. That's what tipped me off."

"It's how I create permanent magic, and it was the only way to break through the demon's defenses."

"So, you don't do that often? Create new magical talents, that is."

"No. Just tiny bits of magic here and there. If I created too much, too many powers, I would draw attention to myself. My signature would change. It'd be impossible to hide how much magic I had. There's no limit to what I can create."

"If you wanted, you could become the most powerful Magica in the world."

"Theoretically."

Concern shadowed his voice. "You'd be hunted. The Order would never let someone with that power run free. Too dangerous."

"Exactly. They caught us once, and tried to use us for our magic." It sucked when your own government hunted you. "Which is why I've kept my secret so long." I shivered. "But this time, the consequences of inaction were too great."

"You had this plan all along." There was something in his voice that I couldn't interpret.

"I knew it was a possibility."

"I'd have liked to have known the truth, but I understand."

I looked at him. "I know. It's dangerous when only one person knows the plan."

He nodded.

"I'm sorry I killed the demon out from under you this time. Now that I know you take them for the High Court of the Angels, maybe I could have let you have him. But the potion that the Devyver gave us…" I shuddered at the memory. "It created a horrible connection between the demon and me. As long as he was alive, I'd feel it. I couldn't live like that."

"I understand." A wry smile kicked up the corner of his

mouth. "If I keep hanging around you, I might have to give up on ever getting my target."

I looked at him, finally feeling like he was looking at me with something other than suspicion. In fact, it looked a lot like understanding. "So, you still want to hang around me?"

"I've never met an ice queen I liked more," he said.

I chuckled. "But what does that mean for us? Like, dates?"

Did I have time for dates? I needed to figure out what the group in Grimrealm was up to. Why they were targeting Magic's Bend.

"Sure. As long as I'm spending time with you, I don't care what we call it."

I smiled, my chest warming. "Well, I'm planning to figure out who the bastards in Grimrealm are. And stop them."

"Sounds like a good first date."

I smiled even more broadly. This was going better than I could have hoped. Maybe the icy side of my personality hadn't driven off all hope of connection with anyone other than Mari.

"I'd like that." I thought for a second. "And um, you can call me Aeri."

"Aeri?"

"It's my real name. Aerdeca is me, too, but it's the public me. Aeri is the private me."

"Aeri." I could hear the smile in his voice. "I like that."

I looked at him and smiled. There was heat in his eyes, and it immediately ignited in my stomach.

At the same time, we leaned toward each other. His lips pressed firmly to mine, and my head swam. The heat exploded inside me as I kissed him, every inch of me lighting up with pleasure.

Declan's lips slowed, and I pulled back.

His face was pale and tinged slightly green.

My stomach dropped. "Oh fates. Are you all right?"

"Fine." His voice sounded rough, and he definitely looked like he was in pain.

"You're not." A chill of horror raced over my skin. *Oh no.* "The nullifying magic that I created. It's affecting you."

This is what Nara the PyroSeer had said back in Nottingham. When she'd bound me in flame and said that Declan and I would be torn apart, *this* had to have been what she was talking about.

"What?"

"It's a side effect of the power I created to stop the demon. It represses the magic of anyone I touch, which makes them feel sick. Like their soul is leaving their body."

Touching me made him feel like he was losing his soul.

Declan met my gaze, a dark understanding dawning on his face.

I drew backward. *Shit.*

I'd just found him, and I could never touch him again.

THANK YOU FOR READING!

I hope you enjoyed reading this book as much as I enjoyed writing it. Reviews are *so* helpful to authors. I really appreciate all reviews, both positive and negative. If you want to leave one, you can do so on Amazon or GoodReads.

If you'd like to learn a little more about the FireSouls (Cass, Nix, and Del), you can join my mailing list at www.linseyhall.com/subscribe to get a free copy of *Hidden Magic*, a story of their early adventures. Turn the page for an excerpt.

EXCERPT OF HIDDEN MAGIC

Jungle, Southeast Asia
  Five years before the events in Ancient Magic

"How much are we being paid for this job again?" I glanced at the dudes filling the bar. It was a motley crowd of supernaturals, many of whom looked shifty as hell.

"Not nearly enough for one as dangerous as this." Del frowned at the man across the bar, who was giving her his best sexy face. There was a lot of eyebrow movement happening. "Is he having a seizure?"

"Looks like it." Nix grinned. "Though I gotta say, I wasn't expecting this. We're basically in a tree, for magic's sake. In the middle of the jungle! Where are all these dudes coming from?"

"According to my info, there's a mining operation near here. Though I'd say we're more *under* a tree than *in* a tree."

"I'm with Cass," Del said. "Under, not in."

"Fair enough," Nix said.

We were deep in Southeast Asia, in a bar that had long ago been reclaimed by the jungle. A massive fig tree had grown over and around the ancient building, its huge roots strangling the stone walls. It was straight out of a fairy tale.

Monks had once lived here, but a few supernaturals of indeterminate species had gotten ahold of it and turned it into a watering hole for the local supernaturals. We were meeting our contact here, but he was late.

"Hey, pretty lady." A smarmy voice sounded from my left. "What are you?"

I turned to face the guy who was giving me the up and down, his gaze roving from my tank top to my shorts. He wasn't Clarence, our local contact. And if he meant "what kind of supernatural are you?" I sure as hell wouldn't be answering. That could get me killed.

"Not interested is what I am," I said.

"Aww, that's no way to treat a guy." He grabbed my hip, rubbed his thumb up and down.

I smacked his hand away, tempted to throat-punch him. It was my favorite move, but I didn't want to start a fight before Clarence got here. Didn't want to piss off our boss.

The man raised his hands. "Hey, hey. No need to get feisty. You three sisters?"

I glanced at Nix and Del, at their dark hair that was so different from my red. We were all about twenty, but we looked nothing alike. And while we might call ourselves sisters—*deirfiúr* in our native Irish—this idiot didn't know that.

"Go away." I had no patience for dirt bags who touched me without asking. "Run along and flirt with your hand, because that's all the action you'll be getting tonight."

His face turned a mottled red, and he raised a fist. His magic welled, the scent of rotten fruit overwhelming.

He thought he was going to smack me? Or use his magic against me?

Ha.

I lashed out, punching him in the throat. His eyes bulged and he gagged. I kneed him in the crotch, grinning when he keeled over.

"Hey!" A burly man with a beard lunged for us, his buddy beside him following. "That's no way—"

"To treat a guy?" I finished for him as I kicked out at him. My tall, heavy boots collided with his chest, sending him flying backward. I never used my magic—didn't want to go to jail and didn't want to blow things up—but I sure as hell could fight.

His friend raised his hand and sent a blast of wind at us. It threw me backward, sending me skidding across the floor.

By the time I'd scrambled to my feet, a brawl had broken out in the bar. Fists flew left and right, with a bit of magic thrown in. Nothing bad enough to ruin the bar, like jets of flame, because no one wanted to destroy the only watering hole for a hundred miles, but enough that it lit up the air with varying magical signatures.

Nix conjured a baseball bat and swung it at a burly guy who charged her, while Del teleported behind a horned demon and smashed a chair over his head. I'd always been jealous of Del's ability to sneak up on people like that.

All in all, it was turning into a good evening. A fight between supernaturals was fun.

"Enough!" the bartender bellowed. "Or no more beer!"

The patrons quieted immediately. Fights might be fun, but they weren't worth losing beer over.

I glared at the jerk who'd started it. There was no way I'd take the blame, even though I'd thrown the first punch. He should have known better.

The bartender gave me a look and I shrugged, hiking a thumb at the jerk who'd touched me. "He shoulda kept his hands to himself."

"Fair enough," the bartender said.

I nodded and turned to find Nix and Del. They'd grabbed our beers and were putting them on a table in the corner. I went to join them.

We were a team. Sisters by choice, ever since we'd woken in a field at fifteen with no memories other than those that said we were FireSouls on the run from someone who had hurt us. Who was hunting us.

Our biggest goal, even bigger than getting out from under our current boss's thumb, was to save enough money to buy concealment charms that would hide us from the monster who hunted us. He was just a shadowy memory, but it was enough to keep us running.

"Where is Clarence, anyway?" I pulled my damp tank top away from my sweaty skin. The jungle was damned hot. We couldn't break into the temple until Clarence gave us the information we needed to get past the guard at the front. And we didn't need to spend too much longer in this bar.

Del glanced at her watch, her blue eyes flashing with annoyance. "He's twenty minutes late. Old Man Bastard said he should be here at eight."

Old Man Bastard—OMB for short—was our boss. His name said it all. Del, Nix, and I were FireSouls, the most despised species of supernatural because we could steal other magical being's powers if we killed them. We'd never done that, of course, but OMB didn't care. He'd figured out our secret when we were too young to hide it effectively and had been blackmailing us to work for him ever since.

It'd been four years of finding and stealing treasure on his behalf. Treasure hunting was our other talent, a gift from the dragon with whom legend said we shared a soul. No one had seen a dragon in centuries, so I wasn't sure if the legend was even true, but dragons were covetous, so it made sense they had a knack for finding treasure.

"What are we after again?" Nix asked.

"A pair of obsidian daggers," Del said. "Nice ones."

"And how much is this job worth?" Nix repeated my earlier question. Money was always on our minds. It was our only chance at buying our freedom, but OMB didn't pay us enough for it to be feasible anytime soon. We kept meticulous track of our earnings and saved like misers anyway.

"A thousand each."

"Damn, that's pathetic." I slouched back in my chair and stared up at the ceiling, too bummed about our crappy pay to even be impressed by the stonework and vines above my head.

"Hey, pretty ladies." The oily voice made my skin crawl. We just couldn't get a break in here. I looked up to see Clarence, our contact.

Clarence was a tall man, slender as a vine, and had the slicked back hair and pencil-thin mustache of a 1940s movie star. Unfortunately, it didn't work on him. Probably because his stare was like a lizard's. He was more Gomez Addams than Clark Gable. I'd bet anything that he liked working for OMB.

"Hey, Clarence," I said. "Pull up a seat and tell us how to get into the temple."

Clarence slid into a chair, his movement eerily snakelike. I shivered and scooted my chair away, bumping into Del. The scent of her magic flared, a clean hit of fresh laundry, as she no doubt suppressed her instinct to transport away from Clarence. If I had her gift of teleportation, I'd have to repress it as well.

"How about a drink first?" Clarence said.

Del growled, but Nix interjected, her voice almost nice. She had the most self control out of the three of us. "No can do, Clarence. You know... Mr. Oribis"—her voice tripped on the name, probably because she wanted to call him OMB—"wants the daggers soon. Maybe next time, though."

"Next time." Clarence shook his head like he didn't believe

her. He might be a snake, but he was a clever one. His chest puffed up a bit. "You know I'm the only one who knows how to get into the temple. How to get into any of the places in this jungle."

"And we're so grateful you're meeting with us. Mr. Oribis is so grateful." Nix dug into her pocket and pulled out the crumpled envelope that contained Clarence's pay. We'd counted it and found—unsurprisingly—that it was more than ours combined, even though all he had to do was chat with us for two minutes. I'd wanted to scream when I'd seen it.

Clarence's gaze snapped to the money. "All right, all right."

Apparently his need to be flattered went out the window when cash was in front of his face. Couldn't blame him, though. I was the same way.

"So, what are we up against?" I asked.

The temple containing the daggers had been built by supernaturals over a thousand years ago. Like other temples of its kind, it was magically protected. Clarence's intel would save us a ton of time and damage to the temple if we could get around the enchantments rather than breaking through them.

"Dvarapala. A big one."

"A gatekeeper?" I'd seen one of the giant, stone monster statues at another temple before.

"Yep." He nodded slowly. "Impossible to get through. The temple's as big as the Titanic—hidden from humans, of course —but no one's been inside in centuries, they say."

Hidden from humans was a given. They had no idea supernaturals existed, and we wanted to keep it that way.

"So how'd you figure out the way in?" Del asked. "And why *haven't* you gone in? Bet there's lots of stuff you could fence in there. Temples are usually full of treasure."

"A bit of pertinent research told me how to get in. And I'd

rather sell the entrance information and save my hide. It won't be easy to get past the booby traps in there."

Hide? Snakeskin, more like. Though he had a point. I didn't think he'd last long trying to get through a temple on his own.

"So? Spill it," I said, anxious to get going.

He leaned in, and the overpowering scent of cologne and sweat hit me. I grimaced, held my breath, then leaned forward to hear his whispers.

As soon as Clarence walked away, the communications charms around my neck vibrated. I jumped, then groaned. Only one person had access to this charm.

I shoved the small package Clarence had given me into my short's pocket and pressed my fingertips to the comms charm, igniting its magic.

"Hello, Mr. Oribis." I swallowed my bile at having to be polite.

"Girls," he grumbled.

Nix made a gagging face. We hated when he called us girls.

"Change of plans. You need to go to the temple tonight."

"What? But it's dark. We're going tomorrow." He never changed the plans on us. This was weird.

"I need the daggers sooner. Go tonight."

My mind raced. "The jungle is more dangerous in the dark. We'll do it if you pay us more."

"Twice the usual," Del said.

A tinny laugh echoed from the charm. "Pay *you* more? You're lucky I pay you at all."

I gritted my teeth and said, "But we've been working for you for four years without a raise."

"And you'll be working for me for four more years. And four

after that. And four after that." Annoyance lurked in his tone. So did his low opinion of us.

Del's and Nix's brows crinkled in distress. We'd always suspected that OMB wasn't planning to let us buy our freedom, but he'd dangled that carrot in front of us. What he'd just said made that seem like a big fat lie, though. One we could add to the many others he'd told us.

An urge to rebel, to stand up to the bully who controlled our lives, seethed in my chest.

"No," I said. "You treat us like crap, and I'm sick of it. Pay us fairly."

"I treat you like *crap,* as you so eloquently put it, because that is exactly what you are. *FireSouls.*" He spit the last word, imbuing it with so much venom I thought it might poison me.

I flinched, frantically glancing around to see if anyone in the bar had heard what he'd called us. Fortunately, they were all distracted. That didn't stop my heart from thundering in my ears as rage replaced the fear. I opened my mouth to shout at him, but snapped it shut. I was too afraid of pissing him off.

"Get it by dawn," he barked. "Or I'm turning one of you in to the Order of the Magica. Prison will be the least of your worries. They might just execute you."

I gasped. "You wouldn't." Our government hunted and imprisoned—or destroyed—FireSouls.

"Oh, I would. And I'd enjoy it. The three of you have been more trouble than you're worth. You're getting cocky, thinking you have a say in things like this. Get the daggers by dawn, or one of you ends up in the hands of the Order."

My skin chilled, and the floor felt like it had dropped out from under me. He was serious.

"Fine." I bit off the end of the word, barely keeping my voice from shaking. "We'll do it tonight. Del will transport them to you as soon as we have them."

"Excellent." Satisfaction rang in his tone, and my skin crawled. "Don't disappoint me, or you know what will happen."

The magic in the charm died. He'd broken the connection.

I collapsed back against the chair. In times like these, I wished I had it in me to kill. Sure, I offed demons when they came at me on our jobs, but that was easy because they didn't actually die. Killing their earthly bodies just sent them back to their hell.

But I couldn't kill another supernatural. Not even OMB. It might get us out of this lifetime of servitude, but I didn't have it in me. And what if I failed? I was too afraid of his rage—and the consequences—if I didn't succeed.

"Shit, shit, shit." Nix's green eyes were stark in her pale face. "He means it."

"Yeah." Del's voice shook. "We need to get those daggers."

"Now," I said.

"I wish I could just conjure a forgery," Nix said. "I really don't want to go out into the jungle tonight. Getting past the Dvarapala in the dark will suck."

Nix was a conjurer, able to create almost anything using just her magic. Massive or complex things, like airplanes or guns, were outside of her ability, but a couple of daggers wouldn't be hard.

Trouble was, they were a magical artifact, enchanted with the ability to return to whoever had thrown them. Like boomerangs. Though Nix could conjure the daggers, we couldn't enchant them.

"We need to go. We only have six hours until dawn." I grabbed my short swords from the table and stood, shoving them into the holsters strapped to my back.

A hush descended over the crowded bar.

I stiffened, but the sound of the staticky TV in the corner made me relax. They weren't interested in me. Just the news, which was probably being routed through a dozen techno-witches to get this far into the jungle.

The grave voice of the female reporter echoed through the quiet bar. "The FireSoul was apprehended outside of his apartment in Magic's Bend, Oregon. He is currently in the custody of the Order of the Magica, and his trial is scheduled for tomorrow morning. My sources report that execution is possible."

I stifled a crazed laugh. Perfect timing. Just what we needed to hear after OMB's threat. A reminder of what would happen if he turned us into the Order of the Magica. The hush that had descended over the previously rowdy crowd—the kind of hush you get at the scene of a big accident—indicated what an interesting freaking topic this was. FireSouls were the bogeymen. *I* was the bogeyman, even though I didn't use my powers. But as long as no one found out, we were safe.

My gaze darted to Del and Nix. They nodded toward the door. It was definitely time to go.

As the newscaster turned her report toward something more boring and the crowd got rowdy again, we threaded our way between the tiny tables and chairs.

I shoved the heavy wooden door open and sucked in a breath of sticky jungle air, relieved to be out of the bar. Night creatures screeched, and moonlight filtered through the trees above. The jungle would be a nice place if it weren't full of things that wanted to kill us.

"We're never escaping him, are we?" Nix said softly.

"We will." Somehow. Someday. "Let's just deal with this for now."

We found our motorcycles, which were parked in the lot with a dozen other identical ones. They were hulking beasts with massive, all-terrain tires meant for the jungle floor. We'd done a lot of work in Southeast Asia this year, and these were our favored forms of transportation in this part of the world.

Del could transport us, but it was better if she saved her power. It wasn't infinite, though it did regenerate. But we'd learned a long time ago to save Del's power for our escape. Nothing worse than being trapped in a temple with pissed off guardians and a few tripped booby traps.

We'd scouted out the location of the temple earlier that day, so we knew where to go.

I swung my leg over Secretariat—I liked to name my vehicles —and kicked the clutch. The engine roared to life. Nix and Del followed, and we peeled out of the lot, leaving the dingy yellow light of the bar behind.

Our headlights illuminated the dirt road as we sped through the night. Huge fig trees dotted the path on either side, their twisted trunks and roots forming an eerie corridor. Elephant-ear sized leaves swayed in the wind, a dark emerald that gleamed in the light.

Jungle animals howled, and enormous lightning bugs flitted along the path. They were too big to be regular bugs, so they were most likely some kind of fairy, but I wasn't going to stop to investigate. There were dangerous creatures in the jungle at night—one of the reasons we hadn't wanted to go now—and in our world, fairies could be considered dangerous.

Especially if you called them lightning bugs.

A roar sounded in the distance, echoing through the jungle and making the leaves rustle on either side as small animals scurried for safety.

The roar came again, only closer.

Then another, and another.

"Oh shit," I muttered. This was bad.

~~~

Click here to join my mailing list at www.linseyhall.com/subscribe and get a free copy of *Hidden Magic*.

AUTHOR'S NOTE

Thank you for reading *Dragon Blood!* If you have read any of my other books, you might be familiar with the fact that I like to include historical places and mythological elements. I always discuss them in the author's note.

There were a few interesting elements in *Dragon Blood.* First, the pub in Nottingham is based upon a pub called the Ye Olde Trip to Jerusalem, which was established in 1189 according to the current owners. It is built against the side of Castle Rock, upon which sits Nottingham Castle. The pub is attached to several caves carved out of the soft sandstone, and patrons can sit in tiny rooms built right into the earth. The pub name is a reference to the Holy Wars that were being fought during the time that the pub was first established. Though there is no documentation to verify that the pub was in fact established in 1189, the caves in the pub were possibly used as a brew house for the castle and may date to around 1067, when the castle was built.

In the book, I modified the name of the pub to be Ye Olde Trip to Brigadoon. I wanted a magical take on the name, and Brigadoon is a magical Scottish village that rises out of the mists for one day every year. The concep came from a 1947 musical with the same name. It was made into a movie in the 1950's.

The island of Eleuthera is a real place in the Bahamas that is inhabited by many kind people (no supernaturals that I know of, but then, they probably wouldn't reveal themselves to me anyway). There are many caves on the island, and the pirates' cave was based upon those. The pink sand beach that the siren led them to was inspired by French Leave Beach, which has beautiful pink sand made from the conch shells that are so common in the ocean around the island.

Aeri's fondness for the scientific names of marine life was apparent during the shark scene. *Galeocerdo cuvier* is the Tiger shark and *Carcharhinus leucas* is the Bull Shark. These are two of the most dangerous types of sharks, and they do happen to live in the Bahamas, but I should note that under most circumstances, sharks are not dangerous. They do not seek humans out as food, and most incidences of shark bites are due to the shark feeling confused or threatened. I'm still scared of sharks, though.

In this book, there were three scenes scenes inspired by Die Hard. Did you spot them? They were the elevator scene, the glass room scene, and the dangle-the-villain-off-the-roof scene.

One of the most dangerous scenes in the book—the one where Aeri jumps off the boat to cut the weeds away from the propellor—was inspired by my mother. When I was young, my parents had a sailboat named *Bonnie Doon* (if you ever check the publishing company for my books, you'll notice that we named it after the sailboat). The *Bonnie Doon* had a propellor, and one night, a rope became tangled around the blades as we were powering through Sodus Bay, in Lake Ontario. It was dark out, and the water was cold, but we weren't going anywhere if someone didn't cut the rope off.

Of course my mother volunteered. One of my most formative memories is of my mother, wearing her teal swimsuit, climbing down into the water with a knife between her teeth. My mother is pretty badass.

I think that's it for the history and mythology in *Dragon Blood* —at least the big things. I hope you enjoyed the book and will come back for more of Aeri and Mari's adventures.

ACKNOWLEDGMENTS

Thank you, Beń, for everything. There would be no books without you.

Thank you to Jena O'Connor and Lindsey Loucks for your excellent editing. The book is immensely better because of you!

Thank you to Orina Kafe for the beautiful cover art.

ABOUT LINSEY

Before becoming a writer, Linsey Hall was a nautical archaeologist who studied shipwrecks from Hawaii and the Yukon to the UK and the Mediterranean. She credits fantasy and historical romances with her love of history and her career as an archaeologist. After a decade of tromping around the globe in search of old bits of stuff that people left lying about, she settled down and started penning her own romance novels. Her Dragon's Gift series draws upon her love of history and the paranormal elements that she can't help but include.

COPYRIGHT

Made in the USA
San Bernardino, CA
16 June 2020

73381386R00149